SCYTHE - SPECIAL EXTENDED EDITION

EDITION

BOOK ONE OF THE DIMENSION DRIFT

CHRISTINA BAUER

COPYRIGHT

Monster House Books
Brighton, MA 02135
ISBN 9781946677259
Second Edition

CONTENTS

NEW APPENDIX OF TOTALLY AWESOME GOODIES

STANDARD APPENDIX OF STUFF THAT'S STILL PRETTY COOL

DEDICATION

For All Those Who Kick Ass, Take Names
And Read Books

COLLECTED WORKS

Dimension Drift

Dystopian adventures with science, snark, and hot aliens
1. Scythe
2. Umbra
3. Alien Minds
4. ECHO Academy
5. Justice
6. Slate

Angelbound Origins

About a quasi (part demon and part human) girl who loves kicking butt in Purgatory's Arena
1. Angelbound
2. Scala
3. Acca
4. Thrax
5. The Dark Lands
6. The Brutal Time
7. Armageddon
8. Quasi Redux
9. Clockwork Igni
10. Lady Reaper

Angelbound Offspring

The next generation takes on Heaven, Hell, and everything in between
1. Maxon

Angelbound Lincoln

The Angelbound experience as told by Prince Lincoln

Fairy Tales of the Magicorum

Modern fairy tales with sass, action, and romance

Pixieland Diaries

Sassy pixie Calla loves elf prince Dare. Too bad he hasn't noticed her. Yet.

Beholder

Where a medieval farm girl discovers necromancy and true love

This is a completed series.

SCYTHE

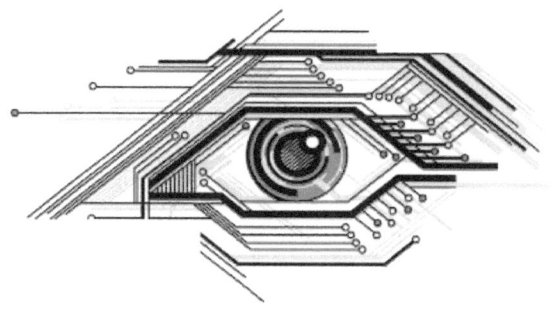

.

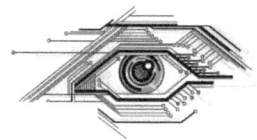

CHAPTER 1

NOT LONG NOW.

Up ahead, a tiny concrete tower rises from the darkened hilltop. *Guardhouse #83.* I scan the gravel road before me. Everything is deserted, quiet, and perfect. Despite the chilly night air, a rush of excitement warms my limbs. Most days, I'm a teenage she-hermit who lives for my basement laboratory. But in this moment, I'm my best self: a science prodigy-for-hire whose inventions secure my family's safety. And if a little thievery is involved? Well, that just makes me a lot badass.

In other words, time to steal for Mom and science.

Marching to the guardhouse, I stop before the intake window. There's no need to announce myself; motion detectors will activate the auto-guard. Seconds later, a mechanical buzz sounds as florescent lights click on, revealing an animatronic woman sitting at a fake desk. Like most auto-guards, this one is less than perfect, what with her chipped plastic skin, frayed blue uniform, frizzed-out hair, and single functioning eye. Raising her head, she addresses me through the Plexiglas.

"You have reached guardhouse #83 for Reclamation Center Massachusetts-1," she says. "The manufacture of new goods is reserved for the military, so we sort, clean, and refurbish old items from landfills."

To kill time, I adjust the loose straps on my backpack. This auto-guard won't interact with me until her welcome spiel is over. Sadly, animatronic speeches at Reclamation Center Massachusetts-1—also called RCM1—always take a while.

With jerky movements, the auto-guard gestures to the monitor embedded in the outer concrete wall. *Here comes the slide show.* Images appear on the screen, showing endless rows of long metal buildings stretching off to the horizon. "Since our founding in 2107, RCM1 has processed more than three million objects across two thousand warehouses. It is now 11:43 pm. How may I be of service?"

That's my cue. All the blah-blah-blah is done.

"I need to check in for my shift," I say.

Which is a total lie.

In truth, I'm visiting RCM1 because I'm building a scientific tool called a *magnetic enhancer* for one of my customers. Why? To punch holes in time and space, you need massive amounts of magnetic energy. Once my enhancer's complete, that process will be a ton easier. At this point, all my invention needs are some *dark matter brackets* and that's it. Fortunately, when it comes to unusual supplies, RCM1 never fails.

"Initiating employee identification sequence," states the auto-guard.

With those words, a long steel tube extends from the concrete wall. I lean in so my eye almost touches the metal. *Almost* is the key word here. I don't even want to think about the quarter-inch of black goo that encircles the tube's end. *Who knows where THAT came from?* A burst of light follows; my retina is scanned.

"Identification complete," she announces. "You, Wisteria Roberts, are sixteen years old and a resident of Reformed New England. Five feet, five inches tall. Brown hair and eyes. You worked at RCM1 full-time between the ages of six and twelve."

All of that's true, except for my name. Wisteria Roberts is an alias; I'm really Meimi Archer. More fun facts about yours truly: I collect oddball alarm clocks, care for my mother, and have regular dreams where I gain superpowers and watch over a cute guy from another planet. *I know, strange.* I'm also a decent computer hacker. In fact, I broke into the RCM1 mainframe seven years ago. Since then, there've been five system upgrades. Yet all my back doors and secret subroutines have stayed 100% valid. *Yay me.*

The auto-guard tilts her head. "You worked here with your older sister, Regina Roberts. Is she checking in with you today?"

"No, Luci—I mean, Regina—isn't here. She's..." I stop myself before saying the word *dead*. "She's just not here," I finish quickly.

My heart sinks. My sister Luci moved to the Boston Dome ages ago. Once there, she became a casualty of the new plague. Four years have passed since Luci died. A weight of sorrow seeps into my bones. After so much time, I shouldn't deeply mourn my older sister's death. Even so, the pain stays as fresh and cutting as if it happened yesterday.

The auto-guard's one good eye flashes with orange light. It's a sign she's still processing my identity profile. "You, Wisteria Roberts, are not a current RCM1 employee, even on a part-time basis. Please step away from the guardhouse."

Now that I'm logged in, I have pre-coded passphrases for such occasions. "Launch super-awesome chick subroutine." As backdoor phrases go, it's not the best. But in my defense, I wrote this code when I was nine.

As the subroutine begins, the auto-guard gives me a somewhat creepy smile. "How's it hanging, girlfriend?"

I grin right back. *That's what I'm talking out. Now I have full access to any system within RCM1.*

"The usual," I reply. "I'm working on a science project for a grouchy customer." He's also a stone-cold killer, but I don't add that part in. "Got any dark matter brackets in stock?"

Once again, the auto-guard's eye flashes orange. "Dark matter brackets may be found in warehouse 942, row 63, bin 13. There are 37 in stock at cost of 100 credits each."

"Temporarily reduce that price to zero and get me four brackets."

The auto-guard's head ticks from side to side. "One moment."

For the record, I'd rather buy these parts officially. Unfortunately, that's not an option. My mother isn't mentally stable, so the government —what we call the Authority—wants to *cleanse* her. That's government-speak for an early death, either from a gun blast or by being fed to a genetically enhanced attack animal. *Not on my watch.* To keep Mom safe, she and I live far outside the government's tracking systems. That's crazy expensive. Projects like my magnetic enhancer help pay the bills. Trouble is, doing any scientific work without government approval is a crime, and RCM1 reports every official purchase to the Authority. All of which brings me back to the auto-guard, illegal hacks, magnetic enhancers, and thievery.

Mitigating factor: I do make anonymous donations to RCM1 in the value of whatever I take, so there's that.

"Price temporarily reduced for one transaction only," says the auto-guard. "Setting aside four brackets now." The automaton's head keeps clicking at odd angles while it performs this function. Somewhere over in warehouse 942, a spider bot—essentially a foot-tall mechanical minion—places my brackets onto a pick-up table by the front door.

After a few seconds, the auto-guard speaks again. "Four functional brackets are now on reserve."

"Display other items in 942." Might as well see what else I can grab.

The monitor scrolls through names of various scientific devices.

Atomic stabilizers? Already have too many.

Quantum chasers? Forget it. Quark trackers work so much better.

Refurbished monolith? That would be awesome, but it's also the size of a refrigerator. Not exactly backpack friendly. And I don't have forever to fart around here.

I'm about to tell the auto-guard to stop when I see it.

1982 era SW AC with DV action.

My pulse speeds with all kinds of happy. I collect specialty alarm clocks, and this is one I've stalked for ages. "Pause, please."

"Listing stopped."

"Does warehouse 942 *actually* have a circa 1982 Star Wars alarm clock with vocal Darth Vader action?"

"Correct. One such item in stock. Row eleven, bin 507. Ten credits."

I smile my face off. This is like finding a picture of Einstein in a tankini; I never thought it was possible. *What a great day.*

"Reduce price to zero," I command. "Then add to my order."

"Acknowledged. Do you require a transport platform to warehouse 942?"

"No, it's faster if I walk." Like everything else here, transport platforms at RCM1 are rickety at best. Plus, 942 isn't too far away.

On the outer wall, the computer monitor stops listing items. Instead, the screen fuzzes over with unreadable text.

I frown. *That's strange.*

Leaning in, I scan for details. The only legible word is *alert*. When I worked here, those mostly concerned new landfill shipments.

"Is something wrong with tonight's delivery?" I ask.

"The next shipment is right on schedule. Precisely at midnight, no fewer than 84 hovercraft will arrive to dump fresh landfill. Contents will then be cleaned, sorted, and any usable items refurbished or recycled as soon as possible. It is now 11:51 pm. Every worker has reported for duty at the unloading towers."

"So tonight's delivery is fine." I'm still stuck on that alert message.

"Fine as sunshine," replies the auto-guard. I loaded about a hundred sayings into this subroutine. What can I say? I was nine and bored.

I nibble on my thumbnail and think through this news. Hovercraft deliveries always take place at midnight. That's why it's my favorite time to steal: all the RCM1 workers are miles away from the warehouses. And while the human workers are busy, RCM1 security relies on drones called Tetras. Imagine a shoebox with four helicopter-style rotors slapped on top of it and that's a Tetra. Pretty useless. My dark outfit—including boots, jeans, and hoodie—will easily hide me from their video scanners.

Even so, a chill of unease moves up my back. Although everything seems fine, something nags me, like a wire isn't screwed down tightly enough.

Best to double-check.

I tap the computer monitor. "I'm still seeing an alert. What is that?"

"The Authority released a general warning regarding the Lacerator."

I lift my brows. "The Lacerator, as in their new genetically enhanced attack animal?" I've seen the newsfeed articles. The Lacerator is the latest addition to what the Authority calls its Horde, which are killer monsters that get rid of undesirables. Meanwhile, the threat of those same creatures keeps everyone else in line.

"Affirmative. That's the same Lacerator," replies the auto-guard.

This is such bad news. No one knows what the Lacerator looks like, mostly because victims don't live to share details. The bodies always have puncture holes and claw marks. Hence the name Lacerator. *Nasty.*

Only one thing to do next.

"Launch amazing subroutine for providing detailed info. Area of interest: Lacerator and RCM1."

Moments later, pictures of hacked-up bodies fill the outer monitor. I wince. *Well, that's never leaving my head.*

"Additional information located," states the auto-guard. "Over the past twelve days, the Lacerator has routinely escaped confinement. Each time, it visits RCM1. During the last invasion, worker casualties resulted."

My insides twist with anxiety. The Lacerator at RCM1? That's seriously not-good, and for three key reasons. First, those poor employees. Working here is bad enough without getting minced to death. Second, RCM1 isn't too far away from the abandoned factory where Mom and I live. *Yikes.* And third, the Lacerator hitting RCM1 means the Authority could get interested in my favorite spot for hard-to-get parts.

Which leads to my next question. "How does the Authority plan to deal with this, if at all?"

Let's be honest. This is western Massachusetts. Everyone who lives or works out here is considered *undesirable*. We don't get plumbing or electricity, let alone police to fight off killer monsters.

"The Authority wishes to study the Lacerator's habits," explains the auto-guard. "A scientific expedition has been dispatched to RCM1 to investigate."

I bob my head and think this through. *One expedition. That's not too terrible.*

"When are they due?" I ask.

"Since most attacks happen after midnight, the expedition arrives within the next two hours."

I take it back. That's totally horrible.

Tension knots up my limbs, but I force myself to stay calm. Two hours is more than enough time. Plus, what do I care about some scientific expedition? It's not like they can cause me trouble. What will they do? Beaker me to death?

"Who's in this expedition?"

"One scientist," replies the auto-guard.

My shoulders slump with relief. "That's great."

"And to protect the scientist, Mercenaries of Righteous Enforcement will also be present. You may know these warriors as the Merciless. Displaying supplemental video."

I stifle a groan. *Everyone knows the Merciless.*

Fresh video appears on the screen. Merciless warriors march down Newbury Street, their *gash guns* gleaming in the false sun of the Boston dome. Skull-like helmets top their black body armor, all of it fashioned to resemble charred bones. A sick taste fills my mouth. The Merciless are screened to be tall, handsome, and card-carrying sociopaths.

Merciless Captains also have an extra pal along: an attack beast trotting at their side. Most of these monsters are pony-sized mixtures of wolf, crocodile, and bat. The Horde.

At this point, things aren't looking good here. Even so, there still may be a chance to salvage this. I need more information.

"Where will the expedition go?" After all, RCM1 is huge. Chances are, the Merciless will end up miles away from warehouse 942.

"The expedition plans to inspect warehouses 127, 559, and 935."

My breath catches. I've hit every one of those warehouses for parts ... and all within the last three months. Even worse, warehouse 935 is not too far from 942, my destination for this trip. And the Lacerator shows up after midnight, which is my favorite time to stop by.

The temperature around me seems to spike about twenty degrees. It's an effort to keep focused.

Stay calm, Meimi. Keep asking questions.

"What can you tell me about those warehouses? Are there any similarities tracked in the system?"

As a scientist, I'm not a superstitious person. Even so, I cross my fingers.

Please, don't let the similarity be me.

The auto-guard stares into empty space for what feels like a millennium. "Similarity detected," she states at last.

And then, nothing.

A long pause follows while the automaton blinks and that's it. I make a mental note to tweak the code in this subroutine. Asking so many questions is giving me a headache.

"And?" I prompt. "What's the similarity?"

"Recently, these warehouses were all visited by the same person, Regina Roberts."

Shock reverberates through my system. "Regina Roberts? Did you say Regina Roberts?"

"That is correct. Is there a malfunction in my voice output?"

"No, it's just that Luci Archer—I mean, Regina Roberts—is my sister. She worked here with me at RCM1, remember?" I don't add in the part about her dying. For some reason, saying it out loud makes the loss too real.

"Providing supplemental surveillance per subroutine. Here you go, honey."

Fresh video flashes onto the monitor before me, showing an aerial view from a Tetra drone. Although the scene takes place at night, I make out someone tall and slim with long white-blonde hair. Her orange cloak flaps behind her as she steps into a warehouse. The woman's face isn't visible, though.

Could that really be Luci?

For a long moment, I can only stare at the auto-guard. *Luci is alive? No way that's correct.* At the same time, part of me wants my sister back so badly, I could scream.

"Update coming in." The automaton's head ticks more quickly than ever before. "Merciless warriors will arrive at RCM1 in twenty minutes."

A knot of panic tightens my throat. *Twenty minutes?*

Okay, I'm enough of a scientist to accept facts here. This caper is toast. I should run for it. NOW. Problem is, my customer's a maniac, as in a seriously psychotic killer who murders anyone that misses a shipment. Even worse, my deadline for this magnetic enhancer is just hours away.

Sweet mother of science.

Mom isn't super-mobile. That said, maybe I could boost a transport for us to escape. But to where? My customer is none other than the Scythe, the most powerful crime lord around. He'll find us no matter what.

Yet he might not discover us right away ...

Taking a half-step backward, I get ready to bolt. Then I stop. *What am I doing?* Screw the Scythe. No way am I pulling up roots; I still have twenty minutes left. Grabbing stuff from RCM1 warehouses is my specialty.

I lift my chin and steel my nerves. *This is totally do-able.* Refocusing on the auto-guard, I give another command. "Make sure my stuff is ready for immediate pick up."

"Acknowledged."

"Shut off the super-cool girl hacker subroutine." The auto-guard slumps forward as my passphrase erases all traces of this conversation. I glance at my watch. Midnight on the nose.

No time to lose.

Hoisting my backpack higher, I run toward warehouse 942.

Between the Lacerator, Merciless, and my killer customer, I have plenty to obsess about. Even so, I can only seem to focus on one thought.

My sister Luci may be alive.

And somehow, she and I are mixed up with the Lacerator.

Sweet mother of science indeed.

CHAPTER 2

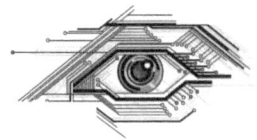

PUMPING MY ARMS, I race down the gravel path toward the RCM1 main campus. Minutes fly by. The stench of bleach and rot grows strong. A thin moon hangs in the cloudless sky, casting a blue glow over the landscape. In every direction, lines of metal warehouses hug the earth. As I speed along, there are no signs of Tetra drones or people. *Perfect.* I glance at my smart watch.

12:07 am.

Pushing myself, I run even faster. By the time I reach warehouse 942, I'm a sweaty mess. Approaching the metal door, I activate the data panel and enter my skeleton key code. The entrance unlocks with a soft click.

I'm in.

As soon I cross the threshold, jolts of excitement move though my limbs. The warehouse interior is dark, which is fine with me. No point attracting attention with extra light. The place is also huge, empty, echo-y, and creepy as hell. My blood warms with excitement.

Is it terrible that I love stealing stuff in the dark? Maybe, but I'll enjoy it anyway.

Slipping a small flashlight from my backpack, I click the device on. A thin beam of brightness cuts across the warehouse, showing long rows of wall-like shelves that stretch from floor to ceiling, creating a labyrinth that fades off into the darkness.

The scene holds a surreal quality that reminds me of my strange dreams. Only unlike my night visions, I'm awake and acting in the world. In this moment, anything feels possible. I could even believe in my power to visit another planet so I can watch over some hot alien guy.

But I digress.

Angling my beam, I find a silver table by the front wall. Dozens of spider bots crawl across the surface, positioning different cardboard boxes. I scan the names atop each package, stopping when I read one in particular.

Delivery for: Coolest Chick Ever.

That's me, all right. Or at least, that's how I saw myself when I was nine and wrote this subroutine. Scooping the container from the table, I open the top. Four Y-shaped wires sit inside. These may look simple, but a lot of tech is crammed in them.

Dark matter brackets. Yes.

A larger box sits beside the first. I grin. That's my new alarm clock. No way will I open this now; that's something Mom and I always share. Holding my flashlight in my teeth, I slip both containers into my bag. While I'm there, I search the backpack for different options that might help my escape ... just in case.

Insect drones? *No, those are better over miles of distance.*

Acid grenades? *Good for breaking through walls; not okay for people.*

Chem darts? *Hmm. Those could help.*

I lift two darts from my pack. The thin vials contain clouds of liquid tranquilizer. Toss them to the ground and—WHOOSH—a blue haze appears that makes everyone fall asleep (not me; I've been immunized.) I grip a dart in each hand. From a distance, they'll look like pens or something. *Perfect.*

Ready to go.

Stowing away my flashlight, I hoist my backpack onto my shoulders once more. With silent steps, I follow the front wall until my fingertips brush the door handle. Fresh adrenaline streams through me. Pulling my hoodie low, I grip the handle, open the door, and step outside.

Oh, no.

Blinding light sears into my retinas, blocking the scene before me. The exterior world appears as a single sheet of brightness. Blinking quickly, I clear my vision. My surroundings slowly come into focus.

What I see isn't good.

Maybe I should have run when I had the chance.

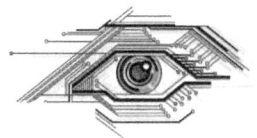

CHAPTER 3

A DOZEN Merciless guards stand in a semicircle before me, all aiming their gash guns in my direction. Ouch. Those things are worse than regular firearms since the bullets explode grenade-style on impact. My body numbs with shock. Even if I toss the chem darts now, the Merciless are known for their reflexes. With so many warriors, the chances one will hit me are about 100%.

Not liking those odds.

In the center of the group, there stands a wispy man who's about five feet tall. His white lab coat hangs loosely around him. Tufts of gray hair encircle what's an otherwise-bald head. Small round glasses sit atop his thin nose. I've seen pictures of this guy before. *Doctor Godwin.* He runs the Authority's program for genetically enhanced animals. In other words, this dude runs the Horde.

Huh. So Godwin is the solo scientist for this expedition? He's a total muckity-muck. Higher ups like him never leave the Boston Dome.

My stomach sinks. There's only one reason why Godwin would hike out to the sticks for research. Hell, there's only one reason Godwin does anything: he's planning another citizen's cleansing.

Every fact from past cleansings runs through my mind. A foul taste creeps into my mouth. If my guess is right, the next cleansing will feature both the Lacerator and western Massachusetts. Why else would Godwin visit here in person?

That's bad news for everyone I know. That said, most people practice how to conceal themselves from cleansings. I'm talking slipping behind fake walls, disappearing into hidden crawl spaces, that kind of thing. But my mother has her fav spot by the window and pitches a fit if she can't sit there. Not exactly helpful when you want her to hide.

I lock my back teeth in frustration. Normally, cleansings only hit the Boston Dome and its suburbs. This far away, we've always been safe.

"Keep holding your fire, soldiers," Godwin says in a sinister whisper. "My pet appears interested in our dark-clad guest."

For the first time, I notice how Godwin clasps a small black container against his chest. I'd think he holds a jewelry box, except it's made from subtly shifting fibers. I draw my brows together in contemplation. Containers made from moving threads? I've never heard of tech like that before.

Even so, something about those fibers seems oddly familiar. I've witnessed that kind of tech before, but I can't place where. Could it be from one of my dreams? It's possible. I get some of my best invention ideas from those visions.

The dark box shimmies in Godwin's hands, interrupting my thoughts. "Quiet, my beastie." He keeps pawing at the container, which is super creepy. "My pet has nothing to fear from you, does he?"

I give the doctor a little nod. Best not to antagonize the evil guy with twelve killer-helpers who's toting around a questionable container.

The box shimmies again. Godwin makes a tsk-tsk noise. "Ah, my poor Lacerator. You don't like your cage, do you?"

Despite the horror of this situation, the scientist in me becomes intrigued. Rumor is, the Lacerator is huge. How would you fit a massive attack beast inside something that small? The non-scientist in me screams, *run for your life!* Only I can't. The Merciless are still focused on me. If I move, they'll blast my brains out.

That's when it hits me. The next few seconds could be my last. A chain reaction of not-so-happy thoughts erupts through my mind.

What have I done with my life? I hide out in a basement, take care of my mother, and invent techie stuff. I've never been kissed (I don't count the incident in second grade.) I rarely see my friends, since that involves leaving my inventions and lab. Sure, I've kept me and Mom alive, but there's *surviving* and there's *living*.

I haven't really lived.

And now I'm about to die.

That realization hits me, hard. The knowledge seeps through my soul in ways I hadn't expected. A single thought overtakes my mind.

To live, I need to change.

Within my deepest being, some sleeping part of me kicks to life. The sensation is both familiar and peculiar. It's familiar because of my dreams where I use special powers. Not that I remember the details of those when I awaken, mind you.

Problem is, I'm not asleep.

I'm very much awake, and things are all too real.

Something about me is actively changing. I can only hope it doesn't get me killed.

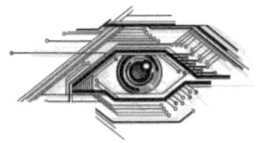

CHAPTER 4

AN ODD, high-pitched ringing fills my ears. I scan Godwin and the Merciless. This is loud stuff, but no one else reacts. Whatever this sound is, it's a noise only I can detect.

That's weird.

Once more, I contemplate my dreams of superpowers and cute aliens. I don't remember specifics of those night visions, but I do know that in them, I wield some kind of special ability. And in this moment? The sensation that those dreams are becoming reality turns even stronger. Deep inside me, pieces of my soul snap and shift.

Panic jolts through my nervous system. *My soul is snapping? Shifting? What the WHAT?*

Scientist-Me seems to hover outside my body for a moment, watching Regular-Me stand rigid before the Merciless. The noise disappears while some black particles materialize around my body. Like with the noise, no one except me seems to notice them.

And they're particles.

Seriously?

Now my soul is shifting AND there's flying grit that only I see? GAH.

Even more particles appear. Now the haze becomes so thick, no one should miss it. I check Godwin and the Merciless once more. Do they notice any of this particle action?

Not at all.

Like with the noise, this is something only I can perceive.

And it's a bunch of flying particles.

Time to reassess my situation.

At this point, I see two options. One, I'm totally insane. Based on my mother's history, that's quite possible. Two, my inventions often poke around in other dimensions and universes. Maybe I picked up something along the way and—whatever that *something* may be—it's been manifesting in my dreams. Now that same thing's trying to help me escape. With option one, I'm pretty much doomed no matter what I do. But option two? If I play along, I might just live.

Option two it is.

More things alter within my soul. Synapses connect. Energies sync. Abilities focus. Great mental cogs whir for the very first time. All the particles around me vanish. Images flash in my head.

Darkness.

Shifting threads of black filament.

A cascade of dark particles.

No question about it. These mental pictures are coming from *inside* that black box. *This is the Lacerator's view.* I take in a shaky breath. Somehow, I'm looking through the Lacerator's eyes, assuming he has them. How would that work, exactly? Before I can contemplate the answer, new emotions flood through me. They aren't mine.

The burn of fury.

An ache of hunger.

A longing so sharp, it's painful.

And finally, the soft chill of calmness.

Once more, I'm certain these emotions come from the Lacerator.

A plan forms. No, *forms* isn't the right word. The scheme appears in my head as a series of images sent to me from the creature.

Image one. The golden container opens.

Two. I speak a command.

Three. The Merciless run away.

Four. I escape.

The creature is using pictures to communicate a plan. In this scheme, the Lacerator wants to get loose, scare the warriors, and enable me my escape.

Nice work, Lacerator!

Now you'd think in this situation, I'd just agree to the creature's plan and get started.

Nope.

One of the great benefit-slash-curses of being me is that I always have an opinion. Always. Even with Merciless guards pointing guns at my face and a genetically enhanced attack animal talking to me telepathically.

In this case, I want to perfect the Lacerator's plan, so I send my new buddy a mental image of my chem darts, hoping the creature understands.

Let's include these in my escape.

After all, some Merciless may hold their ground, no matter how scary the Lacerator looks. With my monster acting as a distraction, I'll have a few precious seconds of surprise that I can use to my advantage. There should be enough time to chuck a chem dart or two. A fresh picture appears in my head. Again, this isn't my creation.

Flash. An image of me tossing chem darts like a pro.

The meaning is clear. My new friend agrees with my suggestion. *Great.*

The Lacerator communicates again, but not with pictures this time. Instead, an electric charge of joy courses through my limbs. I'm taking that as: *let's get started.*

I totally agree.

Still keeping my hoodie low, I gesture to Godwin. "Why don't you set the Lacerator free? I'd love to meet him."

Godwin's thin nostrils flare. "What an interesting test for our little beastie. Do you want to come out?" The box rattles more fiercely than ever. "I can see that you do. Let's try an experiment."

Little by little, Godwin opens the small container. My breath catches as a single dark claw peeps over the box's edge. Then another. Both talons are shrouded in mist, like the creature itself isn't solid. Then I remember my vision from when I was looking inside the box.

Particles. That's what the Lacerator is made from.

And just a few moments ago, I was surrounded in particles as well.

That settles it. The Lacerator uses these particles to connect with my mind. Part of me screams how this isn't normal. These are particles, for crying out loud. *Run, Meimi!* I try to move; my feet stay rooted to the spot. My body feels like part of something else.

Or rather, part of *someone* else.

Strangely enough, that realization only brings a fresh wave of comfort. This time, I'm not sure if it's coming from the Lacerator or me. Even so, I'm all in.

The creature and I are connected. It wants me to escape.

More particles rise from the container, forming a dark cloud before Godwin. This time, it's something he can clearly see, considering how he's staring right at the particle cluster while a small smile rounds his thin lips. Based on how a few of the Merciless tremble with fear, they see the beginnings of the monster, too. *Interesting.* Maybe the Lacerator can control when particles are visible.

The specks shift, taking the shape of a great beast, one that's seven feet tall with dinosaur-style plates down its back. The creature's thick arms end in clawed hands that scrape the earth. Its skull-like face is long, with hollow eyes and a wide jaw lined with rows of knife-sharp teeth. Everything about the beast is solid and yet semi-transparent, reminding me of grit trapped in amber.

The Lacerator.

Quick as a whip, the creature rounds on Godwin, trying to slash the doctor through with its talons. Nothing connects. Every time the Lacerator gets within inches of Godwin's body, the container flashes with purple light. A force field then appears around the doctor—a haze of violet brightness that hovers just above Godwin's skin. Each attack follows the same pattern: an attempted slash from the Lacerator, a flash of purple light from the box, and a violet-colored force field that protects Godwin.

Fresh emotions pour through me. Again, none of them are my own.

White-hot rage.

Bone deep humiliation.

A craving for revenge.

Whatever the Lacerator may be, I know one thing: it loathes Godwin.

"Now, now," coos Godwin. "Be a good little Lacerator. We both know you can't attack me while I hold this." The doctor raises the box in his hands.

The Lacerator pauses, his semi-transparent body quivering with fury. Tilting his head back, the creature lets out the mother of all roars. The howl is so strong, objects in nearby warehouses crash to the ground. Even the black armor of the Merciless rattles.

The doctor doesn't so much as flinch. "Why don't you say hello to our new friend, my pet?"

At this point, it strikes me that my escape plan could be one big con. After all, don't some creatures lure their prey right before attacking? Maybe the Lacerator is the Venus fly trap of bloodthirsty monsters. Bands of worry tighten around my chest.

Inch by inch, the Lacerator rounds on me. Every cell in my body freezes. Fresh feelings stream through my soul.

The magnetic pull of interest.

An ache of longing.

The electric thrill of joy.

The beast towers above me, arms raised, and claws extended.

Although its pose is menacing, I sense no threat from the Lacerator.

Without question, I move forward with our plan. As the image instructed me, I give a command.

"Go after the Merciless," I order.

The Lacerator's body explodes into a cloud of particles. Thousands of tiny projectiles tear through the Merciless. Armor, helmets, bodies, and gash guns—nothing stops the onslaught. The particles rip through the warriors in a thousand places at once. Moving in unison, all twelve soldiers crumple to ground, dead.

I blink hard, not believing what I'm seeing.

This can't be right.

But the Merciless really aren't moving. Blooms of red blood seep out over their armor.

Oh, yeah. These dudes are totally dead.

Some corner of my mind—the part that's a normal human being—screams in horror. I just asked the Lacerator to *go after the Merciless*. The vision had them running away, not transformed into Swiss cheese.

There isn't time to worry about that, though. Godwin's still alive. Plus, the doctor controls the Lacerator with that black container. Maybe he can order the creature to come after me, too.

I need to escape and fast.

Launching into the next part of the escape plan, I chuck the chem darts into the ground. As each vial hits the earth, a plume of blue smoke rises into the air, creating a wall of haze that's impossible to see through. Even better, it contains a sedative that works almost instantly, smells like lilac, and doesn't affect me. My friend Zoe made these. She's a genius with chemicals.

A moment later, the smoke vanishes. Doctor Godwin lies on the ground, snoring up a storm. He grips the container tightly against his chest.

I quickly scan the scene. There are warehouses, dead bodies, a sleeping doctor, and a gravel walkway.

No sign of the Lacerator.

Then I notice it.

The doctor's dark container rattles furiously. New emotions tear through me. Like before, they aren't mine.

A chill of fear.

The zing of panic.

A heavy weight of grief.

That's the Lacerator, I know it.

I step toward the doctor, my arms outstretched. A single thought echoes through my head.

Grab that container.

Deep voices sound in the distance, breaking up my thoughts.

"Backup needed, warehouse 942!"

"Bring more gash guns!"

"Hurry! Hurry!"

I'd know those particular tones anywhere. Only the Merciless have their speech electronically enhanced to sound extra low and evil. More are coming and fast.

Their cries snap me back to reality. Am I out of my mind? Hanging around here is suicide. And what would I do with a pet Lacerator anyway? The plan was always for me to escape solo. I shake my head and refocus.

It's beyond time to leave.

So I run like hell.

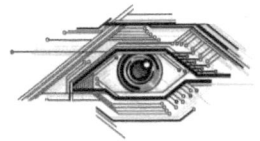

CHAPTER 5

MY HELL-RUNNING CONTINUES until I've left RCM1 far behind. Soon I reach Old Williamstown, or what's left of it. Time was, thousands of people lived here. Then came the so-called War of Liberation—where the Authority defeated the United Americas government—and this place got leveled, along with most of the continent. Now it's nothing but rubble.

Keeping up my frantic speed, I rush to the outskirts of town until —yes!—I reach the ruins of an old gas station. Like everything else these days, the building is totally crushed. Red bricks lay in heaps all around. A smashed-up gas pump slumps sideways on the gravel. Good thing there's a metal hatch around back; it leads to a secure basement. Much as I'd love to race home, I need to stop there.

And worse, I must call the Scythe.

Why am I pausing in my run-a-thon to chat with a crime lord, or to be accurate, with his minion Fritz? I can't risk the Authority finding out about me and the massacre at RCM1. Right now, I'm a girl in a hoodie. But if they ID me? Mom and I are toast. But to hide us requires hacking that's beyond my skills, mostly because it involves more than computers. You need to know people in low places.

That means the Scythe and Fritz.

Fortunately, this hidden basement is a great spot for calls. Yanking up the metal hatch, I find a familiar set of stairs leading into the ground. A minute later, I'm in the basement itself, pacing around a dusty room while typing an emergency access code into my smart watch. This lets Fritz know I need to talk.

Seconds tick by as I wait for Fritz to reply. My mind whirls through the events at RCM1. What happened to me? There's been research about people who become so panicked, they lift up freight cars or get visions of the future. But I've never heard about anyone creating a mental link with a monster made from particles before.

My watch plays a few bars of *Another One Bites The Dust*, breaking up my thoughts. That specific ringtone means Fritz is taking my call. I exhale. Soon a thin beam of light pours out from the side of my watch, casting a hologram image on the opposite wall of the concrete room.

It's video of Fritz, and he's beating someone up.

My stomach twists. *Damn, I want to help Fritz's latest victim.* From experience, I know my best option here is to distract Fritz himself.

"Hey, there." I clear my throat. Twice.

Fritz is a mountain of a man, what with his stocky build, square face, and white spiked-up hair. He always wears overalls and speaks with a German accent. That is, the accent shows up when other people are around. It's totally fake; Fritz thinks it makes him seem more ominous.

Like the guy needs help. Sheesh.

The hologram shows a prone body curling up on the floor before Fritz. Since the victim's facing away from me, all I can tell is that the man's wearing a suit. Fritz boots the dude once more in the stomach. I wince.

"This better be good," says Fritz. "As you can see, I'm busy."

"Will you stop kicking that guy while we talk? He's unconscious."

"Who says that?"

"You're not using your fake German accent, and you only do that when we're alone. Which means the guy is out. Enough already. Please. We need to chat."

"I've got a better idea. Why don't you come to my office? You know the Scythe doesn't like electronic comms."

"Come on. It's an emergency."

Fritz gives the guy one last kick and then turns to me. "What do you need *this time*?"

For a big bad killer, Fritz can be a total baby. If I let him start whining, he'll never stop.

"Hey," I counter. "Don't give me attitude. I make you and the Scythe a ton of credits." In fact, I started building their illegal science gizmos when I was eleven. That was the same year Fritz became my handler. Dad died right after I was born, so Fritz is actually the closest thing I have to a father. Not a comforting thought.

"So?" asks Fritz. "Deliver that magnetic enhancer by 6 am. That gives you around five hours. Make it happen."

"I will. Only one part left."

"Then don't bother me." Fritz steps nearer to the holo-camera in his office, the device that's projecting his image. Walking closer means Fritz plans to shut off our link.

"Hold up there. I just ran into the Merciless, Doctor Godwin, and the Lacerator at RCM1."

Fritz pauses. Even in projected form, his ice-blue eyes bore into mine. "Define *ran into*."

"The Merciless are dead, I left Godwin unconscious, and the Lacerator is back in its container cage. Can you fix this?"

Fritz's voice lowers. "Define *fix*."

"Erase any traces of my presence. I wore my hoodie but you could still see the bottom half of my chin. That might identify me."

"Did you speak?"

"A sentence or two."

"That's more than enough for an ID and you know it." Fritz folds his massive arms over his barrel chest. "This'll be tricky."

No question what Fritz's *arm-folding routine* is about. He wants to know what's in it for him.

"I can pay you," I offer. "The Scythe promised me 3,000 credits for my magnetic enhancer. Clean up this mess, and you can keep 1,500."

Fritz glares for a long minute. As the moments tick by, my palms turn slick with sweat. Sure, I have other customers who could clean this up, but I'd have to sleep with one eye open for the rest of my life. When it comes to erasing messes, no one's more connected than the Scythe.

Finally Fritz speaks. "Should I know *how* you walked away from a bunch of dead Merciless guards and one passed-out Godwin?"

"It's like this." My mind races, trying to think how to slowly introduce what's easily the craziest experience of my life. "I think Godwin's planning a citizen's cleansing in this area."

"Not a chance. The Scythe pays big bucks to keep the Authority out of our backyard."

I lift my brows, impressed. I had no idea the Scythe did that, but it makes sense.

"Try again," says Fritz.

On second thought, there's no point lying or beating around the bush. Fritz can sniff out untruths easily, especially from me. And the man has zero patience. "I developed a telepathic connection with the Lacerator and it helped me escape."

Fritz stares at me for a long second. Then, he bursts out in laughter. "So you had a psychotic break and don't remember how you got free."

I shrug. "That's possible, too."

"You think?" asks Fritz. "Oh, that story is just too good. Now I have to help you."

I grin. "Thanks."

"But there's a condition." He jabs his hefty finger in my direction. "You move into one of our safe houses."

I set my fist on my hip. "You know I can't do that."

"Why? The Scythe's condos tricked out with the latest tech. Plus they're totally off-grid."

"But Mom can't join me there."

Fritz sniffs. "Your mother's been catatonic for years."

A jolt of protective energy moves up my torso. "That's not true. She home-schooled me for ages. Even now, Mom still has plenty of good days. She's all the family I've got."

I actively ignore the thought that Luci may be alive. *That's just too much.*

"No one watches over *undesirables* anymore, family or otherwise. Let the Authority take care of your mother."

"You know what that means. They'll kill her."

"So what? They terminate everyone who doesn't meet their standards. Why should she be any different? Deal's off."

I ball my hands into fists. There's no explaining family to Fritz. The guy believes in the Authority's motto, *empathy is weakness.* Time to appeal to his sense of greed instead of duty.

"What if you keep all 3,000 credits? That's a good offer. My magnetic enhancer is unique. Nothing else on the market even comes close. And I can't finish it when I'm dead."

Fritz slowly rubs his square chin. "And you'll still deliver the enhancer by 6 am?"

"Absolutely."

"And I keep every credit?"

"That's what the science girl said."

"Then I'm in." He lets out another dramatic sigh. "Although, I really wish you'd go into a safe house, Meims. You worry me sick."

I shake my head. *You worry me sick.* For Fritz, that's a tsunami of fatherly sentiment.

"Oh, and too bad about the 3,000 credits," he adds with a chuckle. "Sucker." This time, Fritz marches forward and shuts off the comm link entirely. The basement around me goes dark.

Despite the inky blackness surrounding me, I can't help but smile. *Too bad, my butt.* I always build back-up copies of my inventions. If the Scythe won't pay me 3,000 credits, I'll find another buyer who will.

Next stop: my home and magnetic enhancer.

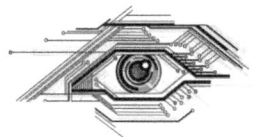

CHAPTER 6

A HALF-HOUR LATER, I march up to the derelict factory where Mom and I live. Old plastic signs hang on cockeyed angles on the brick buildings, all of them reading: *Ozymandias Chemical.* A gentle breeze cools the sweat on my face. The adrenaline rush from my encounters with the Lacerator and Fritz are all long gone. Now I just feel bone tired.

The main factory is a long, two-story affair nested in a labyrinth of smaller structures. If you look carefully enough, you can still see stuff painted on the bricks.

Remember your eye protection.

Caution! Dangerous chemical storage!

All overtime must be pre-approved.

Our entrance sits at the far end of the main building. I approach the rusted door, enter my key code into the alarm system, and step inside. What happens next is more of a reflex than a thought.

Check on Mom.

Right off our entrance, there's a small storage-room-turned-kitchen. It's Mom's favorite spot, so I go there first. Sure enough, she's in her chair by the window, watching bits of trash roll down the cracked sidewalk. Mom's already in her pajamas with a robe tied tightly at her waist. The woman I pay to look after my mother during the day—an older lady named Miss Edith—did her job getting Mom ready for bed.

Speaking of Miss Edith, she sits at her favorite spot at the kitchen table. Miss Edith is a thin stick of a woman with short gray hair and a laser-sharp mind. She sets down her chipped teacup as I approach. "Hello, Meimi. How was basketball practice?"

"Fine."

Miss Edith smacks her lips. "I thought you were attending a late night study session with your friends, Chloe and Zoe."

I pause just inside the kitchen door. Damn. I'd forgotten that I asked Miss Edith to stay late so I could supposedly study.

Think fast, Meimi.

"Here's the thing," I begin. "Zoe, Chloe, and I played basketball for a while. Then, we studied so hard. So, so, so hard. Whew!"

Miss Edith drums her wrinkled fingers on the tabletop. "Really? May I see the books inside that backpack of yours?"

I bite back the urge to groan. Miss Edith will not give up until I answer her honestly. "Okay, I didn't really play basketball or join in a study session. I'm working on another science project for a customer."

"Meimi ..."

I huff out a breath. "We need the money."

"I understand that." Miss Edith rises and puts her teacup in the sink. "You should be in school."

"Technically, the computer systems say I am in school. Every day." *I figured out that hack ages ago.*

"You know what I mean. The schools here may not impart anything useful. Honestly, you could teach them a thing or two. Even so, there's the social aspect to consider. It's not healthy for a young girl to spend hours working in a basement."

"Hey, I tinker in my bedroom too."

Miss Edith sighs. The sound reminds me of how Fritz did the same not so long ago. "Have it your way," says Miss Edith. "But don't expect me to sit here and say nothing."

"I would never." Stepping up, I give Miss Edith a quick kiss on the cheek. She pretends not to smile.

"You're the best," I say softly.

"See you tomorrow, Meimi." Miss Edith waves to Mom. "And you too, Rose."

Mom doesn't reply, but that's typical. My mother needs a few minutes to adjust to change, that's all. Once Miss Edith is gone, I drag a chair beside Mom's.

"Hey, Mom. It's me, Meimi." Scooching closer, I pull out a box from my backpack. "Guess what? I got something new for my collection."

Mom blinks hard. That's her way of trying to focus. For years, we consulted doctors about her condition. No one could figure out what's wrong. In the end, the only thing we know is that Mom becomes catatonic for longer periods every day. Her forehead crumples as she scans the cardboard container in my hands. "Wha ... wha ..."

I finish the sentence for her. "What is this?" I tear the box open. "A Star Wars alarm clock." I gingerly pull out the plastic device, revealing a small plastic Darth Vader statue. A digital clock lies embedded in his chest. So awesome.

Raising her shaking hand, Mom taps Darth's head. "Good." Her eyes crinkle as she gifts me a smile.

My heart warms. *This moment, right here. It's what I love for.*

"R..." Mom strains to form the word. "R..."

"RCM1? Yes, that's where I went to get it. Things got a little crazy there tonight." The auto-guard's report comes back to me in a flash. *Luci may be alive.*

Memories flood my mind.

I'm six and Luci's eighteen. We stand in my old bedroom at our government house in Malden, a suburb of the Boston Dome. The furniture's a mishmash of rickety tables and chairs the government painted yellow. Luci kneels before me. She's all things lovely and elegant as she explains why I won't go to school today. "Mom's having another episode," says Luci. "You'll work with me now, Pumpkin. We'll use pretend names and play clean up." Without question, I follow her out the door. It's my first day at RCM1.

In my next memory, I'm twelve and Luci's twenty-four. This time, we're in the kitchen of our house in Malden. Luci's new fiancée, Josiah, waits outside. Mom sits at the chipped yellow table, looking like an older version of Luci: white blonde hair and aristocratic features. Mother silently stares at the floor while Luci explains that she and Josiah are moving to the Boston Dome. Luci turns to me. "Don't worry, Pumpkin. I'll send you plenty of updates and money." We never hear from her again.

Then I recall a scene from five months later. I'm tossing out old boxes from the Ozymandias Chemical factory. Soon after Luci left, the Authority announced another citizen's cleansing for Malden. Mom definitely would've gotten scooped up, so we moved in here. As I work away, a scream sounds from the storage room we're using as a kitchen. Rushing in, I find Mom sitting by a window, a tablet in her hand. I scoop the device from her palm and read aloud. "Casualties Announced In Latest Wave Of Boston Plague." Scanning the list, I find the names Josiah and Luci DeBurgh.

My world shatters.

Luci is gone.

I grip the plastic clock more tightly in my hands. The question tumbles from my lips. "Do you ever think Luci might still be alive?"

A wild look enters Mom's blue eyes. "Yes."

I lean in closer. This kind of clarity is rare from my mother. "What makes you say that?"

"Convergence."

"That's right, there's a magnetic convergence coming up." With so much excitement, I almost forgot. This particular variety of inter-dimensional storm happens every year around my birthday. Sadly, that's also the day my father died. Needless to say, it's never been a big holiday in our house.

"Convergence," repeats Mom. "Luci."

I frown. "Not understanding you."

"Important!" Mom grips my wrists. "Luci!"

"Okay." In reality, I have no idea what Mom is talking about, but it's pointless to push her for more information. That only makes her more upset.

Instead, I gently pry her hands from my wrists and reset my new Vader clock in its box. I can't sit here with Mom forever; I must focus on other stuff. *Like finishing that magnetic enhancer.* Standing, I gently rest my hand on Mom's shoulder.

"You need some sleep," I say softly. "Let's go upstairs."

Mom follows my guidance and takes to her feet. Leaving our small kitchen, we step out onto the main factory floor. It's an open space that's two stories tall and a quarter-mile long. Every inch is covered in a jungle of vats and pipes. Along the second story, the walls are lined with small offices that overlook the floor, all connected by an open catwalk.

Together, Mom and I step up the spiral staircase to the second floor. We converted two of the chambers up there into bedrooms. The rest are all mini libraries with books I've reclaimed from RCM1. There's a room for computer programming, chemistry, mechanical engineering, you name it. Mom used to love reading new books and quizzing me on stuff. She'd also spend hours inventing in the old chem lab across the factory floor.

Sadly, those days are long over.

Setting my hand on Mom's elbow, I guide her to her bedroom door. My mother's steps are shaky and her eyes unfocused, so it's slow going. Eventually, I help her into bed as well. A tiny window casts a square of light across her frail frame and thin blanket. Mom's shoulders rise and fall in a slow cadence.

A shiver rolls up my spine. *What if Mom gets worse?*

Images flash in my mind. I picture the Merciless guards again, only now they're leading Mom away. A rope of worry tightens around my torso. With a force of will, I shake off the thought.

If Mom gets worse, I'll deal with it then. For now, I have other concerns, like that magnetic enhancer. Turning around, I head out the door and cross the catwalk to my bedroom.

I have a deadline to meet.

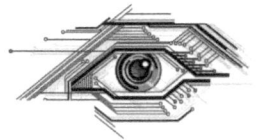

CHAPTER 7

LESS THAN AN HOUR LATER, I'm seated on my bedroom floor. Shelves of specialty alarm clocks line the walls, along with one small cot. I lift my magnetic enhancer from my lap, giving it one last scan. *What a mess.* This thing could be abstract art sculpture called *Wire Octopus Drinks Too Much Coffee.*

I shrug. *Chaotic* is the typical look for my inventions. My stuff is never pretty; it simply works. And this magnetic enhancer just passed all my diagnostics with ease, including the new dark matter brackets. A warm sense of pride seeps through my heart.

It's done.

Tapping my smart watch, I summon Fritz again. Music sounds before his holographic image appears. This time, he isn't kicking anyone to death. Bonus.

"What did I say about electronic comms?" asks Fritz. "Come down to my office."

"I am not hauling my butt around in the middle of the night. Just send a drone. Besides, if you *really* wanted me in the office, you'd never have taken my call."

Fritz's beady eyes glare at me through the hologram. "Show some respect. I just spent hours paying off government officials for you. Even Godwin doesn't remember you now. Can you imagine what that took? And still, you won't follow basic protocol and see me face to face."

The hair on the back of my neck stands on end. *That little revelation from Fritz raises a good question.*

Which I probably shouldn't ask.

Actually, considering how cranky Fritz is, I definitely shouldn't ask this question.

In fact, a younger version of Mom's voice echoes through my memories, saying: *"Meimi Archer, stop asking questions."*

But I can't help it; I ask the question.

"How'd you fix Godwin's memory?"

Fritz's voice lowers. "Never telling you that."

"Did you bribe him to *say* he doesn't remember, or did you use that new memory wipe technology?" I've been dying to learn how that stuff works.

"Meimi, I swear on my grave, the next words out of your mouth better be thanking me for cleaning up your crap. Because if you keep pushing, I'll tell the Scythe you missed your deadline. I've had it."

And although I like asking questions, even I know when to stop. Besides, there are other ways to find out how Fritz fixed Godwin. Something for later.

"Thank you," I say solemnly. "Now, can you please send a drone for this thing? If I go out this time of night, I'll hit thieves or worse. Then you'll have even more trouble to deal with."

Fritz exhales another of his long, put-upon sighs. "Fine."

Seconds later, a tapping sounds. No question what that is. Rising, I cross the room and open my bedroom window. Sure enough, one of Fritz's drones waits outside. *A massive silver hawk.* Swooping inside, the fake bird lands atop my dresser. Once settled, the hawk's belly snaps open to reveal a hidden transport compartment. It's a bit of a squeeze, yet I'm able to get my magnetic enhancer inside.

"All done," I announce. The bird takes off.

The hologram version of Fritz stares at me for moment too long. Genuine regret seems to flash across his face, but it's gone too quickly to be certain. Besides, I'm not convinced Fritz is capable of feeling guilt.

"Bye, Meims." His hologram disappears.

With Fritz gone, I should collapse onto my cot for some well-needed sleep. Plus, I often get those superpower dreams with my mystery guy, so you'd think I'd want to snooze right away. *Not happening.* Instead nervous energy hums through my body. I pace a line on the concrete floor, my thoughts racing. This is how I feel when I leave a Bunsen burner on or a power line ungrounded.

Something isn't right; I just don't know *what.*

Pulling out my data pad, I quickly scan the news feeds. There's nothing about RCM1. *That's good.* Still, I don't allow government spider bots or drones in the factory, so I'm not dialed into the main Authority information line. It's just too risky to break in when there are safer ways to access the same data feed directly. That means one thing.

I'll have to go to school tomorrow. That place is crawling with government tech that I can tap without leaving any incriminating electronic signatures. But that means my hermit-self must come up from her basement lair to interact with other people her age.

Ugh.

My uneasy feeling deepens as my thoughts return to the Lacerator. Maybe that's what has me so cranked up. Did I truly mind-meld with that thing? My scientific brain quickly comes to an answer.

Fritz was right. It was all an illusion.

My brain probably short-circuited due to adrenaline overload. Somehow I escaped that situation and my mind wants the reality of it all to remain a mystery. Got it. When people are pushed to extremes, odd things happen.

With that thought, warm waves of comfort move through my limbs. The more I think about it, the more I know I'm right. There's nothing to worry about between me and the Lacerator.

Finally, I settle into my cot for a serious rest. Soon I'm enveloped in yet another lifelike—and totally amazing—dream. Unlike my waking life, it features a very handsome guy. I won't remember much in the morning, but right now, I'm not complaining.

Ah, dreamland. So much better than reality.

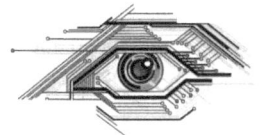

CHAPTER 8

NOW, I have my share of routine dreams. Like showing up to school without any pants. Or getting lost in the maze of vats that cover the Ozymandias factory floor. They're all a little psychedelic too: walls morph, faces change, and noises vanish. You know, the classic dream stuff.

Then there are my night visions of the boy.

And those are incredibly lifelike.

Sure, I can never remember his name when I wake up. In fact, I'm lucky if I can recall a few snippets of anything in the morning. There are superpowers and a hot alien, that's pretty much all I get. But once I'm asleep, like I am right now? I savor every last detail.

His name is Thorne.

This time, my dream of him begins in a small domed room. The walls shimmy and arc, like they're breathing. Then I remember. Everything here is made from shifting fibers.

A jolt of realization hits me. When I saw the Lacerator today, it was contained in a box made of this same stuff. Moving threads.

I look down, seeing a thin haze of blue particles surrounding me. The name of these tiny creatures appears in a flash. *The Sentient.* They're miniature combinations of tech and organic matter that work in a hive mind. For some reason, they keep pulling my consciousness here to another planet. That name becomes clear as well. *Umbra.*

My dream-self then comes to a conclusion that's very different from its waking counterpart. My connection with the Lacerator was real. All of what happened at RCM1 is directly related to these dreams, which are no dreams at all.

Everything is so clear to me in my dreamland. I make a solemn vow.

Remember this in the morning, Meimi. The Lacerator is from Umbra. My power is a connection to the Sentient. All of it is real.

Some small part of me knows this is a long shot. I never remember my dreams during the daytime. Even so, that won't stop me from trying.

My attention focuses back onto the domed room, mostly because of its solo inhabitant. In the center of the round floor there stands Thorne. He's tall and broad shouldered with limbs that are roped with strength. The muscle part is hard to miss since he's bare chested and holding a sword. Thorne has a square face, strong jawline, olive skin, and large blue eyes. He's a little older than I am, maybe eighteen or so. Like always, his hair is cut in short military style.

"Begin," he commands.

The brown threads of the floor come to life, rising up into the shape of a sparring partner. Thorne has fought these before. The partners are computerized battle routines called *wicks*, and they're used for training. Thorne bows to his faceless opponent. The sparring partner does the same.

For my part, I stand by the wall, well out of the action. Thorne never notices me in my dreams. That's fine. I'm just happy to ogle from a distance. I'm not sure why the Sentient take me to Thorne. After so many years of dreams, I'm not sure I care, either. Watching this boy is a balm to my soul. It doesn't matter if I never meet him. We're connected somehow, and in my solitary life, that's enough for me.

Thorne begins a series of warm-up lunges, followed by a speed round of thrusts and parries. His wick keeps pace, which is pretty impressive. All too soon, we're interrupted.

The wall to my right shimmies with more force. The threads making up the panel divide, like curtains that are pulling apart. Through this new opening, another figure walks into the room.

Thorne's Mother, Janais.

She's tall and broad-shouldered, just like her son. Not for the first time, I marvel at her strong cheekbones, copper skin, and long neck. She wears a brown robe made of the same shifting fibers as everything else. The garment's train twists as it follows behind her. A lace-like set of threads weave along her neck.

For a few seconds, Janais watches her son practice. Then she speaks. "Your reaction times are getting better," she says in her deep alto.

Here's what Janais *really* means by that. Thorne has two brothers, Justice and Slate. Wielding the Sentient is the currency of power here in Umbra. Both Justice and Slate command far more Sentient than Thorne.

Justice wields battle Sentient, while Slate controls ones for seeing the future. Thorne wields a little of all four Sentient varieties—black for battle, silver for knowledge, blue for visions, and red for danger—but not enough to perform any major tasks.

Thorne keeps on practicing. Sweat glistens down his back. "Why are you here, Mother?"

"You must convince Justice. Your older brother listens to you."

"Convince him to kill father? No one can do that." Thorne makes another lunge at the wick and misses. Big mistake. The sparring dummy gets a strike in on Thorne's left shoulder. That's the first serious hit the wick has gotten in. I know why. This conversation upsets Thorne, which is totally understandable.

Who wants to kill their own father?

Janais presses on. "That's why the three of you must do it together. You, Justice, and Slate. Be secretive and surprise him." She lifts her chin, but there's no missing the wobble in her voice. Janais cares for her husband. "Your father is suffering. This is the only way to give him peace."

A sense of sadness weighs down my bones. Thorne's father, Cole, is the Emperor of the Omniverse, the universe of universes. As such, Cole acts as both guardian and gardener for the many worlds under his domain. Basically, he prunes back parallel universes that could threaten other worlds. Sadly, the unique set of Sentient he uses for this purpose are eating away his mind. For months now, Janais has pressed for a mercy killing.

Thorne moves into an aggressive set of strikes. The wick steps backward. "Father may be saved yet. Slate thinks there's hope."

"Your baby brother is a dreamer."

"His visions often come true."

"Only when he has them time and again. But Slate only had one vision—just one—where there was a transcendent mate. A brief flash of a single reality where Justice found his transcendent, a mystery woman could match Justice's power, making my eldest son strong enough to defeat Cole without killing him. That's a false dream. Transcendents don't exist."

Thorne strikes a killing blow through the wick's chest. The sparring dummy melts back into the floor. Thorne turns to his mother, pulling in deep breaths from exertion. "But what if Slate's vision is true? Justice could have someone who balances him out. Someone who does—"

"What I thought I could do for your father?" Janais shakes her head.

"I wanted to be his transcendent. I wasn't. There's no such thing, my son."

"My brothers and I are all in agreement. We'll help patrol the omniverse, keeping the worlds safe. That will buy us time to find a transcendent for Justice."

"That won't work," counters Janais. "Cole already fears Justice will assassinate him. He keeps attacking your brother. Soon one of them will perish. You will choose which." She steps closer. "You fight well in a simulation, my son. No one works harder at their studies. But that is all you can do. There are palace servants with more power over the Sentient. The only way your life has purpose is if you convince your brothers to act when the time comes. You must save Justice. He's the eldest. It's his destiny to be Emperor."

Thorne scrubs his hand over his face. "I would never stand by while Justice died."

Janais's head slumps forward with relief. "Don't wait too long, then. And please don't place your hopes in those silly visions from Slate." She snaps her fingers; a section of wall opens up once again. Janais starts to leave; then she pauses once more. "I was harsh before. I know you work hard to compensate for your lack of power. If only you weren't so weak with Sentient, you could have been the greatest Emperor of them all."

Harsh words, but Janais is a harsh empress. It works for her.

With that, Thorne's mother steps out the opening in the wall.

Once she's gone, my vision ends too.

For the rest of the night, I dream that I'm in the Ozymandias factory, searching for a book in one of my libraries. I tear through shelf after self, but the books transform into birds as soon as I pull them free. Even so, I don't stop.

This is important. I must find the right book. It has something to do with the Lacerator. I must remember.

But no matter what I do, I can't recall a thing.

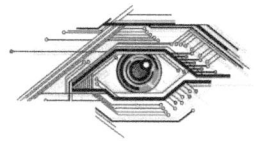

CHAPTER 9

7 AM.

My collection of old Earther alarm clocks goes berserk, right on schedule. I grin into my pillow. These wake-up calls are the best.

"Good morning," cries one clock. "It's Howdy Doody time!"

"Who's asleep in a pineapple under the sea?" sings another.

And finally, the best and newest addition to my collection.

"Luke, I am your wake-up call."

Reaching under my mattress, I pull out my data pad and scan for news. There's still nothing about RCM1. *Yes.* Say what you want about Fritz, the guy does deliver. Then again, my data pad isn't enough total proof. I still must hit school and check the official information streams. Again, that means leaving my hidey-hole of scientific joy and interacting with other kids my age.

Yuck.

Swinging my legs over the side of my cot, I haul my butt out of bed and shut down the alarm clocks. This morning, that task isn't so easy. My fingers keep fumbling over buttons, which comes no surprise. After all, I only got a few hours of sleep. Now it's like my brain is stuffed with cotton balls or something.

So.

Tired.

My woozy head tries to process what's happening. Why was I up so late again? *Oh, that's right.* Quality time with magnetic enhancers and the Lacerator.

Another banner day for Meimi Archer.

Memories knock at the back of my mind. Last night, I had another one of those vivid alien romance dreams. Straining my thoughts, I try to recapture some shadow of what I saw. There was a handsome boy involved and something about the Lacerator, too. No matter how hard I try, I can't recall a single thing.

Oh, well. I can try to remember something later. Right now, school awaits.

Leaving behind thoughts of my dream boy, I drag myself into my regular morning detox shower. The spray smells like rotten eggs and burns your skin, but it's the only way to live out here and not glow with radioactive waste. Afterwards, I apply my chelation balm and slog through getting dressed. The Authority forbids manufacture of new clothing except for the military, so my jeans, boots, and *I Heart Science* T-shirt all sport holes and stains.

Once ready, I half-sleepwalk downstairs to the kitchen. My heart lightens to discover that Miss Edith is here early.

"Morning, Miss Edith."

"Greetings." She takes a long sip of tea while eyeing me carefully. "You're not getting enough sleep again. Neither am I, for that matter. But only one of us went to bed right after we parted." She taps her chest in a way that says, *and that person would be me.*

One thing I love about senior ladies. No bull.

I shrug. "You know how it goes. I had that project to finish." This morning, I'd love to avoid a deep discussion with Miss Edith about my health and side projects for the Scythe. "How's Killer?" That's her cat, as well as a possible segue to a new topic.

Miss Edith takes another long sip before replying. I know her system. She's debating about whether to push me here. At last, she replies. "Killer is up to her old tricks as always. Brought me a dead mouse yesterday."

In other words, she is deciding not to push. *Yay.*

"Sounds yummy." I scoop my school backpack from the floor. This one actually has notebooks and pens inside instead of darts and bombs. "You know the routine," I add. "Take care of Mom. See you after school."

Miss Edith waves to me as I leave. "Say hello to that MacGregor boy," she adds.

"I always do." MacGregor—everyone calls him G—is one of my classmates. We got fake-married in the second grade. It was a recess game and, sad to say, it's the closest I've gotten to dating anyone, before or since. I should stop trying to resurrect that relationship, but I can't seem to help myself.

Leaving the factory behind, I trek through back alleys and side streets until I leave the Ozymandias Chemical complex. Soon I reach Winter's Run, the main town nearby. The area's really cute. The locals have cobbled together new buildings from refurbished bits of stuff. The schools here are collaboratives where families pool resources. Volunteer teachers play by the rules and report all scores to the Authority.

Obviously, this is not where I take classes. If I went to a collaborative, I'd need to give my real name and go to school regularly. Let's just say that doesn't fit my current lifestyle.

Twenty minutes later, I come to my school. In old Earth, this place might be called the Chuck E Cheese of academia. It's an Authority approved, for-profit institution called Learning Squirrel High. And in case you're wondering, *for-profit* means *easy-to-bribe*. The students here are all hiding from the Authority.

Every. Last. One.

Most kids have parents who work for the Scythe. Others are like my best friends, Chloe and Zoe, who attend because their father's terminal cancer makes him an *undesirable*. In a collaborative, the school would have to report parental fitness. But Learning Squirrel is pay-to-play. You *pay*, they *play along*. Zoe and Chloe's father is listed as being in perfect health. I'm registered here as Wisteria Roberts.

In short order, I reach a familiar muddy field before a patchwork of double-wide trailers. *Learning Squirrel High.* Dozens of kids hang out in the central mud pit that's the waiting area for class to start. The moment I step onto the grounds, Zoe and Chloe make a beeline in my direction. They're identical twins—tall and willowy with golden hair—but beyond that, they couldn't be more different. Zoe is a genius with chemicals and sourcing cute clothing. Today, she wears cool black boots and a fitted trench coat that says: *I'm runway bound.* Meanwhile, Chloe sports the coverall look made famous in gas stations everywhere. Her hair stays pulled into two ever-present ponytails. The look totally suits her, considering how Chloe's a genius with all things mechanic.

The twins stomp through the mud and stop before me. I point at Zoe's trench coat. "Why isn't there any mud on you? Did you create some new treatment chem for the fabric?"

"We're not talking about that right now." Zoe tilts her head, making her straight blonde hair fall in a perfect arc over her shoulder. "Chloe and I want in."

I decide to play dumb. "That's right. I haven't been to school in ages. Let me share all the news about Miss Edith."

"Puh-LEASE," groans Chloe. "We saw the Authority newsfeed this morning. They're saying the Sister Rage rebellion broke into RCM1 and killed some Merciless guards. It was a flipping bloody mess."

That's nice language from Chloe, by the way. Normally, she has a potty mouth.

"There is no such thing as a Sister Rage rebellion," I counter. "The Authority made that up so they'd have a fake enemy. And besides ..." I nibble my thumbnail. "Last I checked, there wasn't anything about RCM1 on the news."

"That's because you stay off government channels." Zoe rolls her eyes. "This RCM1 story has *Meimi Archer* written all over it."

Suddenly, I become very interested in the straps on my backpack. "What makes you say that?"

"Come on," groans Chloe. "RCM1 is your number one spot to steal shi—"

"Language," interrupts Zoe.

"To steal stuff," finishes Chloe. She then sticks out her tongue at her sister. I love Chloe.

"About RCM1." I raise my pointer finger. "I always make a donation in the same amount. So it's not really stealing."

"We know that," continues Chloe. "What we're saying is this: You did something that could land you in buttloads of trouble. Zoe and I want the details so we can help."

Emotions battle it out in my nervous system. There's the warmth of gratitude for the fact that I have such amazing friends, followed by the chill of terror that Zoe and Chloe will ever get involved in my vortex of crazy.

"Your mother works triple shifts as a medic," I explain at last. "All she wants is to keep you and your father off grid. I can't pull you into my stuff. That would paint huge targets on your backs."

Zoe frowns. "Because you work for the Scythe?"

I lower my voice. "You really shouldn't say his name out loud."

"Like his criminal ass is some big secret," says Chloe. "You're missing the point. All Zoe and I do is read books, invent stuff, and hide out. There are houseplants who've seen more of the world. We're ready for action. A-C-T-I-O-N."

"Besides," adds Zoe. "Dad doesn't have much longer." Her big blue eyes glisten. "We can't lose you too, Meims."

They both look so open and helpful, I hate to shoot them down. An idea occurs. "I know a way you can help. Luci might be alive. Maybe you can hack into some systems, see what you discover."

Zoe and Chloe share a long look. My heart sinks. I know what that particular flavor of glance means. To them, my revelation is no revelation.

Chloe is first to speak. "About that ..."

"You knew?" I take a half step backward. "How could you keep it from me?"

Zoe moves closer. "We weren't certain, but we had our suspicions."

I fold my arms over my chest. "Still not understanding."

"We want to be supportive," adds Zoe. "But Chloe and I talked it over. There are things about Luci you didn't need to know because..." She taps her chin. "How do I put this?"

Chloe hooks her thumbs into the back pockets of her coveralls. "Here's the deal. If I had a little sister, I'd never make her work in a garbage dump, especially at the ripe old age of ten."

"Or eight," adds Zoe.

"Actually, I was six."

"That's what we're saying." Zoe points at my nose. "You were a child. It makes sense that you'd idealize Luci at that age. But your sister did things that were, well, bad. She's still doing them."

All of a sudden, it's like I'm channeling Fritz. "Define *bad*."

Zoe lifts her chin. "I found some people mentioning Luci and Josiah in chat rooms for Authority workers."

"More like ranting," clarifies Chloe.

My world tilts on its axis. "You're saying that Luci and Josiah are not only alive, but they're working for the Authority? That's not possible."

"How can you know for certain?" asks Zoe. "Will you risk your mother's life on that? Because if you reach out to Luci, she could blow you both in. Right now, your sister doesn't know where you are."

Protective energy rushes through me. "Luci would never place Mom at risk, even if we did tell her where we live."

"I don't know; you should read these rants." Chloe lets out a low whistle. "According to these folks, Luci is an entitled—"

Zoe raises her hand. "Language."

"*Witch with a B*," finishes Chloe. "And Josiah's both handsy and disgusting."

All their insights hit me like so many stones. The stuff written on chat boards is probably just a bunch of rumors. At least, I hope it is. But the point about my working at RCM1 at six? That's totally valid. I'd just never thought about it that way before.

I hug my elbows. "This is super confusing."

"Sorry, Meimi." Chloe winces. "But before you take risks for Luci and Josiah, we thought you should know."

Ding, ding, ding!

For the record, I've never happier to hear the class bell. And I must admit, I did get the information I needed about RCM1 from Chloe and Zoe. I just discovered a whole lot more about Luci, too.

"And we still want in on whatever troubles you," adds Zoe. "You can trust us. We'll help."

And I do trust them. Trouble is, I still trust Luci, too. There must be some explanation for all this. I just have to find my sister and get it.

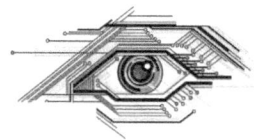

CHAPTER 10

Zoe, Chloe, and I step into the double-wide trailer for science class. A bunch of mismatched chairs are lined up in three rows. MacGregor Jacoby sits up front. He's a total bad boy with his heavy-lidded eyes, black leather jacket, and tousled dark hair. The kid is totally out of my league. I should *not* say hello to him. It's just a recipe for humiliation.

Then again, it's not like I have tons of chances to interact with guys my own age when I'm awake.

I pause by his rickety desk. "Good morning, G."

Did that sound weird? Needy? I have no idea. Math formulas have rules. Guys? Not so much.

G slowly lifts his brows. This kid knows how to work his swagger, all right. "Do I know you?"

"I'm Meimi. We got fake-married in second grade."

"Not ringing any bells." He shifts in his chair. "Wait, you hang with Zoe, right?"

"Sure, she and Chloe are my best friends."

"You think Zoe likes me? Ask her."

This is a reasonable request. Not sure why G can't do it himself, but hey, what I know about men is very little. Cupping my hand by my mouth, I call across the trailer. The twins have seats in the far corner, so it's the fastest way to get the job done. See? Logic at work.

"Hey, Zo! G wants to know if you like him."

For the record, everyone wants to know if Zoe likes them. She's that girl. Best to get the requests done quickly.

"Not interested," says Zoe smoothly.

"She thinks he's a douchebag," adds Chloe.

"Language!" Zoe elbows her sister.

G slowly shakes his head. "Do me a favor, loser. Never talk to me again."

I stagger backward. He asked me for help. I did what he wanted. Now, there's no more confusion for G on the Zoe front. Problem solved. What's up his butt, anyway?

Boys are so confusing.

Crossing the room, I slip onto a chair beside the twins. My face is burning up, I'm so humiliated. I'm not a loser, really. It's just that I plan to make more friends after my next prototype is done. Maybe.

Zoe pats my hand. "Don't worry about that guy. You were just trying to be nice. Chloe set him off. She shouldn't have added the douchebag reference."

"True," says Chloe. She raises her voice as she adds: "G is more of a *dick* than a douchebag."

Zoe sighs. Looks like she's giving up on saying *language* for the umpteenth time this morning.

"Thanks guys," I say, and I mean it.

Unlike boys, girls are the best.

At the front of the room, our teacher looks up from her rusted metal desk. She's a rail of a woman with frizzy brown hair and beady eyes. Although her name is Gertrude Bumgartner, we call her *the Bummer* because, well, that's what she is. You know the tone of voice you use when someone asks you to run upstairs for the millionth time ... and then keeps forgetting what you're supposed to look for? It's a particular kind of whine that mixes resignation and rage. That's how the Bummer speaks *all day long*.

"Morning, class," says the Bummer. She doesn't wait for a reply before continuing. "My data pad says we're having a hologram message today from none other than the Doctor Godwin, leader of the Authority's creature development program."

My skin prickles over with awareness. Godwin is giving us a message, today of all days?

No need to freak out. It's probably just a coincidence.

A spider bot crawls into the trailer, scales up the wall, and perches itself in a top corner. Light sears out from its round body; another hologram appears in the front of the room.

It's Godwin.

"Hello, young people," says the doctor. "I have great news for you today. In response to the latest set of murders by the rebel group calling themselves Sister Rage, our own beloved President, Mother Hope, has authorized me to lead the next phase of our genetic modification and creature development program."

I tilt my head, considering this latest batch of lies. Mother Hope would never hold off on the next phase of developing attack animals. What's Godwin getting at, really?

The doctor straightens the neckline of his lab coat. "For some time, we have sought to create the next generation of both the Merciless and their Horde. We'd set steep deadlines for our scientific team on this project, as well as severe penalties for missing goals. Unfortunately, those scientists failed us. Now we're seeking a new group of brilliant minds to see this project through."

Huh. I may not understand all guys, but Godwin? The dude is transparent to me, it's so obvious what he's up to: his old scientists didn't get the job done, and so Godwin had them killed. Now he's looking for fresh workers from the under-eighteen crowd.

"Therefore," continues Godwin. "We require an elite group of brilliant high school students with malleable minds and a strong work ethic. We have new, uh, technology that can load the needed learning into your minds."

I roll my eyes. *Sure, they can just load in learning.* I've heard about that tech. Maybe it works for one kid in a thousand. For most folks, the process just melts your brain into goo. Everyone knows that it's a lot easier to wipe specific memories away than add new ones.

A chill moves up my arms. At least, I hope everyone knows that. I scan my classmates. No one here would be dumb enough to volunteer, right?

"The standard school year ends on June first," says Godwin. "That's just a few short weeks away. Summer school will then begin at ECHO Academy, which is the world's finest institute for scientific minds. Anyone sixteen to eighteen years old may submit to take aptitude tests for admission to my unique summer program. The more current skills you have in the sciences, the more likely you are to be accepted into the program, and to have success with the knowledge implants."

Zoe pokes my shoulder and mouths two words. *No way.*

I silently reply. *Agree.*

"And here is the best part," continues Godwin. "If you prove valuable to the Authority over the summer, we will provide you with a sponsor family to cover your entire tuition at ECHO." Godwin gestures toward the Bummer. "Don't be shy. Submit your name to your teacher, take our screening tests, and serve the Authority. Thank you."

The light on the spider bot dies out. The image of Godwin disappears.

Slumping over her data pad, the Bummer takes over the speech. "Now I'm supposed to ask for volunteers with some basic skills." The Bummer flicks her finger across the screen some more. "The Authority especially needs those with knowledge of chemistry, mechanics, and drift science." She pokes her tongue in her cheek for a long time.

Danger sign.

The Bummer doesn't often think for herself. But when she does? It's usually accompanied by that *poke your cheek with your tongue* move.

"Wisteria, Louise, and Drillbittina. Don't you three have some science skills?"

My eyes widen. *Definite trouble ahead.*

When it comes to aliases, Wisteria is me, Louise is Zoe, and Drillbittina is Chloe. Sure, we kids call each other by our actual names, but that's because the teachers don't remember our names anyway, whether fake or real. And now the Bummer not only figured out our aliases, but she's also got some ideas on our skills? Scary. Although, to be fair, Chloe did make up her fake name Drill-bit-tina in honor of mechanics, so there's that.

"Wisteria Roberts, we'll start with you. Do you have any particular skills in drift science?"

I do my best *dumb bunny* impression. "Drift science. Whatever does that mean?"

The Bummer lets out the softest of groans. "Let's see what it says here." She starts reading from the data pad. "*The drift* refers to the dimension drift, the arm of science that specializes in how our reality overlaps with others. Things are connected in ways we sense are present, even if we can't detect them." She looks up. "I think it's like, *step on a crack, break your mother's back.* That kind of thing. "

A totally lame description. Drift science is only the coolest thing in any universe.

The Bummer goes on. "Drift scientists create calculations, design equipment, and envision connecting worlds together. The practice combines engineering, quantum physics, computer science, and a little artistry. Some call it the ultimate scientific pursuit."

And we have the best toys. Not that I'm saying those words out loud right now.

"Any of this sound familiar to you?" asks the Bummer.

I scrunch up my face to make it look like I'm thinking. After a decent pause, I reply. "Nope."

"Okay, sounds legit." The Bummer types a few keys. "Next up." She looks to Zoe. "Louise Jones. Any special skills related to chemistry?"

Zoe glances around the room, as if seriously contemplating this question. She also puts in a good pause before speaking. "I use bleach to clean the toilet."

"Thanks for sharing. I'll just type in *no interest*." The Bummer focuses on Chloe. "And Drillbittina Jones. Anything with you and mechanics?"

"I say my entire name while burping. Does that count?" Chloe brightens. "I can demonstrate, if you want."

She can, too.

The Bummer taps her cheek. She's actually considering this. "Nah." She scans the room. "Anyone else looking to volunteer? There's no quota listed, so I don't care either way."

The class is silent. *Excellent.* I wouldn't want anyone to get their brains fried out with those learning implants.

Setting aside her data pad, the Bummer launches into a monotone speech about the periodic table. My eyes flutter with the need for sleep. At some point, science class ends. I spend the rest of the day slumped in a series of chairs, trying to catch some very needed shuteye. It's hard to rest without a deskie-thing to lean on, but I try anyway. Chloe or Zoe poke me whenever it's my turn to say something in class.

I don't perk up again until I'm marching home. Like always, Mom and Miss Edith are in the kitchen. My mother's in her regular chair, but her body trembles with excitement. The moment I step in the room, Mom turns to me.

"Sun. Corona. Convergence. Electromagnetic energy."

Miss Edith shoots me a sympathetic look. "She's been this way all day. I think she needs more sleep."

"Sure thing." Stepping to Mom's side, I guide her toward the door.

As we walk away, Miss Edith wags her bony pointer finger in my direction. "Maybe you should head to sleep early as well."

"That," I say slowly. "Is a brilliant idea."

I can't see Miss Edith any more, but there's no missing the smile in her voice. "I have my moments."

Taking Miss Edith's excellent advice, I set Mom into bed and tuck myself in early as well. It isn't until I'm setting my alarm clocks that I notice the date.

It's my birthday tomorrow. With so much excitement—not to mention the magnetic convergence coming—I forgot all about it. Not that there's much competition. Once the magnetic convergence starts, multiple versions of Earth will encounter massive solar storms at the same moment in time-space. The result will be a magnetic energy spike of massive proportions, if you have the equipment to detect it. Like so much with the universe, it makes things like turning seventeen seem small in comparison.

Ah, science. Always good for putting things in perspective.

Once my clock alarms are all set, I collapse into bed. This time, I fall asleep almost instantly. I don't dream about the boy, though.

That makes me sadder than it should.

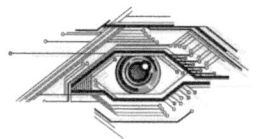

CHAPTER 11

"Ahem."

A voice sounds above me, interrupting my much-needed snooze. Little by little, I force my eyes to open. Mom stands over my bed holding a thermos, moldy picture frame, and plastic bust of Albert Einstein.

That wakes me up, fast.

This must be a dream. After all, my mother is awake, alert, and holding objects over my bed. Plus, she's even wearing one of her old lab coats from her researcher days. The frayed insignia of "United Americas" is still visible on her pocket protector. We're not even supposed to say the name of the United Americas anymore, let alone save themed clothing.

At this moment, the words *total panic* pretty much sum up my life.

"What's wrong, Mom? It's—" I glance at my alarm clocks "—just after 4 am."

"Nothing's wrong, Meimi. I'm merely stopping by for a motherly visit."

"Umm ..."

Shock ripples across my skin. That was a string of coherent words. *From my Mom*. I'd forgotten the sound of her regular voice—it's clipped and deep, the tone of someone who gives orders and expects to be followed. Suddenly, she's the old Mom again. The one who claws science into me with a ferocity that makes mother tigers look like the wimps of the animal world.

Wow. Welcome back.

At this point, I consider Mom's entire visit to be a present, which is perfect considering how it's now officially my seventeenth birthday. Not that I wouldn't like a gift box or a *happy birthday*, but there's no point being greedy. The old Mom being out of her chair and speaking complex sentences is more than enough.

"I brought you some decorations." Mom crosses my bedroom, carefully stepping around the piles of notebooks and circuit boards covering the floor. She pauses by one particularly large knot of wires. "What's all this?"

"You know me. Another project." That's my extra magnetic enhancer. I'd explain all that in detail, but my brain's still stuck on the whole *Mom speaking in full sentences* thing.

"Were you well compensated?"

"Sure." I skip over the part when I traded with Fritz for a favor. "Why else would I do it?"

"You can get wild ideas, Meimi. Sometimes I worry that you'll join some kind of resistance movement, like Sister Rage."

"That's not a real rebellion."

"Maybe not." Her mouth thins to a worried line. "But you still need to do your work—"

"And keep my head down. I remember." Back when Mom was more tuned in, we'd have this conversation all the time. I skip to the big ending since I know Mom will go there anyway.

"The Authority is too powerful," I say in a sing-song voice. "The best anyone can do is hide."

"Correct. Now let's get back to brightening this place up." Mom moves to stand before my rickety dresser. After swiping off all the dust with her forearm, she positions the mashed-up bust of Einstein in a spot of honor.

"Looks great, Mom." Honestly, she could put it anywhere and I'd say something nice. This whole situation is a miracle.

Mom pats Einstein's head and sighs. "Here's why we live off grid. So you know who this man is." She finishes positioning the empty frame. "All done."

There's an obvious question here, which I can't help but ask. "Why an empty frame?"

"It's to remind us that Luci is gone."

My throat tightens. "Right." *As if I could forget.*

The empty frame also reminds me of all the other blanks about Luci. Did Zoe and Chloe tell the truth? I open my mouth, ready to ask if Luci acts like an entitled *witch with a B*, or if Josiah's a nasty creeper. Unfortunately, that line of questioning feels like tossing a sledgehammer through a stained glass window. This moment is simply too lovely to destroy. We can chat about Luci later. If ever.

Mom pulls a piece of white chalk from the pocket of her lab coat and waves it around. "Let's work the drift."

My mouth falls open with shock. "You want me to help you?"

Back when Mom had more lucid moments, she always worked the drift solo because, as she put it: *Meimi, you've a brilliant mind but no stomach for being told what to do.*

In other words, I'm a lot like her.

All of which is interesting since Mom says I take after my father. Maybe that's just in the looks department, though, not temperament. I definitely don't fit with the tall, willowy, and white-blonde thing Mom and Luci have going on. That said, I have to take Mom's word about the Dad-stuff since she didn't keep any pictures of him around. *I know, super suspicious.* But my mother is also semi-unhinged at best, so there's that.

Mom gifts me a gentle smile. "Yes, work the drift with me. I need your help. The convergence has begun and it's simply extraordinary. We're seeing the greatest magnetic storm in a century."

Pieces of the last few days fall into place. My eyes widen. "You're planning something special with magnetic fields."

"Correct again." Mom winks. "I can use those fields to get help."

"Help for what, exactly?"

"Why finding Luci, of course. She's not dead."

Surprise prickles across my skin. "You known that? For how long?"

"I've known for years, I just haven't been able to do anything about it until today."

The words tumble from my mouth. "Did you also know that Luci's an entitled *witch with a B* and Josiah's a creeper?"

Stained glass window, meet sledgehammer. I really need to stop asking every question that comes into my head.

Mom pins me with an honest stare. Like me, she considers facts to be both sacred and shared, even if others don't want to hear them.

Especially if others don't want to hear them, actually.

"Here's the truth as I see it," says Mom. "Before you were born, your father, Luci, and I all lived in the Boston Dome. Truman and I both researched and taught at ECHO Academy."

I blink hard, trying to process this news. My parents once worked at the greatest school for science in the world? That doesn't seem real. All of a sudden, the whole *we lost all our pictures* thing makes sense. Maybe Mom wanted to forget her past. If I were living in an abandoned warehouse in the sticks, I'd certainly be tempted to toss out pictures of ECHO Academy.

"There's more," continues Mom. "After your father died, I left ECHO to work in a private lab. You, Luci, and I then moved to Malden. That wasn't easy for your sister. Luci missed our old life. ECHO is far more glamorous, you see."

"I get that." Everyone's seen images of that campus. It's like a spaceship landed by the Charles River.

"That's why Luci found Josiah so intriguing. He had plans for life in the Boston Dome. I don't know about him being a so-called creeper, but Josiah did make rather large promises to Luci. So yes, Luci had a bit of an attitude sometimes, and yes, I coddled her. Call it a motherly weakness." She lets out a long sigh. "You see, I set up he experiment that killed Truman."

Whoa. Talk about a morning for revelations.

I knew there was some kind of explosion that ended my father's life. That said, I didn't know Mom was part of it. "That's rough."

"I felt so guilty for your father's death and its impact on Luci. I still do. That clouded my judgment."

"Is that why you let Luci take me to RCM1?"

Mom's shoulders slump. "Yes. You weren't learning anything in school, and it seemed so important to Luci that she have company at work. You were always so strong, Meimi. Luci wasn't." Mom's eyes glisten with guilt. "Even so, you shouldn't have been forced to work at such a young age. I'm sorry about that."

My throat tightens with emotion. "You're forgiven, Mom."

A realization hits me. Right here, this morning—it's the most I've talked to my mother in years. Who knows when we'll chat again? I don't want to spend our last conversation crying over the past. "Let's change the subject. How can we find Luci?"

Mom brightens. "Today's convergence gives us options. We can leverage the storm's power to open a stable corridor to another world. Then we can send a message for help. It's an excellent opportunity, team. I mean, Meimi."

Team. That's right. Mom used to have a fleet of assistants. At this point, those people would probably say, *What do you want me to do?* But those folks aren't here. I'm Meimi, and I push back when something doesn't seem right. There are about a million questions I want to ask, most of them science-related. So I whittle the long list down.

"I have two questions."

Mom sighs. "Meimi ..."

"Question number one. Who's going to help us and why?"

Mom's nostrils flare. "Back when we worked at ECHO, some beings from another world asked me and your father for help. They owe us."

If Mom jammed a cattle prod in my side, I couldn't be more shocked.

"Let me get this straight." I raise my pointer finger. "You and Dad were contacted by actual aliens?"

Side note: This is huge. While other kids were playing house, I begged for games like *meet the lizard men from Pluto*. Luci was the only taker, and then it was on the strict understanding that we'd follow up with a round of *Barbie Dream Date*.

Mom gives me the side-eye. "You know the drift. Countless universes exist alongside this one. How can you be surprised?"

I side-eye her right back. "It's one thing to know in theory about aliens. It's another to maybe even dream about them. But it's another-nother to have some actual aliens call your parents. You can't just drop a bomb like that and not expect me to want details."

"I am and I do." Mom's deep voice takes on that rough edge which means one thing: she's about ready to head into the lab without me. Family stories about alien encounters will simply have to wait.

"Second and final question," I say. "You'll call these beings ... how?"

Mom folds her arms over her chest. "We have a language between us. If I toss something with Luci's DNA on it through the corridor, the right person will know how to respond." She pulls a brush out of her pocket. "This has some of Luci's hair. Really, Meimi. We don't have time for this. The magnetic storm won't last much longer and—"

"Stop right there."

"What?" Mom bites off the word.

I hold my arms up, palms forward. "You convinced me. I'll help." I hop out of bed and start scrounging around for relatively clean clothes.

A small smile rounds Mom's mouth. "See you in the lab."

With that, Mom takes off while I uncover a pair of old jeans and a T-shirt in a corner. All the while, my soul feels so light I could cheer.

I'm about to work the drift with Mom. Some small part of me warns that my mother is unstable and getting her anywhere near volatile equipment is too huge a risk, but I overrule that worry.

After all, it's my birthday. My present awaits.

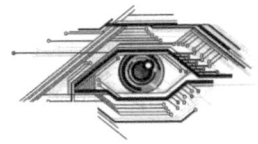

CHAPTER 12

MINUTES LATER, I'm navigating through the forest of vats on our factory floor. Soon, I reach a pair of rusted metal doors on the far-right wall. Written in chipped white paint are the words: *Research Lab—Authorized Personnel Only.*

In my mind, it might as well say, *Mom Only.*

Over the years, I've imagined all the cool tech Mom built inside. Power boosters. Dimensional lenses. Quantum detectors. I invented versions of that same stuff in my basement lab. But my creations got cobbled together in a small storage area. This is a real laboratory: longer than a city block and filled with equipment.

And today I'm going in. After taking in a long breath, I knock on the door.

"You ready for me?" I ask.

"As ever."

I step inside. What I see knocks the breath out of my lungs.

So. Much. Crap.

The space is huge and open. Rows of large chalkboards line the walls, all of them covered in equations. A maze of old Formica tables lie the floor, their surfaces topped with racks of glass vials. Every few yards, there stands a tall machine called a monolith. These can hold all sorts of equipment inside, everything from network routers to dark matter simulators. The ones here look rusted, dusty, and untouched for decades. Most likely, they're in desperate need of upgrades.

In the far corner, Mom sits at a workstation, furiously typing onto a keyboard. Green screen monitors line a partition wall before her. I step up to her side.

"So," I begin. "This lab needs some work, eh?"

Mom keeps typing. "What do you mean?"

"Where are your wormhole regulators? Quantum field windows?" I scan the nearby tabletops. "You don't even have an exotic matter detector."

Mom shrugs. "I get along fine without any of that." She slaps her hand onto the wobbly tabletop. "Damn. This isn't working. At this rate, I'll never tap into enough magnetic energy from the storm. Take a look at this code, Meimi. What do you think?"

My soul swells with pride. This is me and Mom, swapping thoughts in a lab. Love it. Stepping closer, I scan the computer screens. All the data adds up to a single conclusion. "You need a magnetic enhancer."

Mom scrubs her hands over her face. "If one existed, that would be perfect."

"I have one in my room, remember?"

Mom swivels around in her chair, stopping when she faces me fully. "Is it finished?"

I grin. "Oh, yeah."

Mom eyes me for a long moment. I can almost see the doubts swimming through her head. "Bring it here. I'll take a look."

What a day. I'm invited to the lab and Mom needs one of my inventions.

Happy birthday to me.

As I rush back to my bedroom, my steps feel feather-light. Soon I'm back inside my concrete citadel of old Earther alarm clocks. The magnetic enhancer is exactly where I left it. Scooping up the device, I speed-walk back to the lab. Mom's still typing so quickly, I'm surprised she doesn't get a finger cramp. I hand her my creation.

Mom turns the device over while eyeing it carefully. A pang of anxiety moves through my chest. My invention may work, but it really does look like a wire octopus. Will she approve?

At last, Mom speaks. "This is perfect. Well done, Meimi."

My chest could burst with pride. "Thanks."

"So who requests this level of work?" Mom stares at me with her right eyebrow arching upward. She already suspects who booked this particular job.

Here goes. "The Scythe."

"But he's a criminal."

"Who keeps us off grid. It's fine, really."

"It's not fine, and I wish things were different." Mom slumps back in her seat. "My mind." Her voice quivers. "It's not fair to you."

I kneel before Mom's chair so I can get a better look at her. "It really is okay. You took care of me for years. Plus, you taught me how to take care of myself. Everything I know about the drift is thanks to you. Now it's my turn to give back."

Mom gives me a shaky smile. "Well, working for the Scythe has clearly developed your skills." She hands me the enhancer. "This really is top notch."

What a compliment. If I died now, I'd be a happy Meimi.

"I'll pop it on a monolith."

"Place it on the one nearest me." Mom gestures to an area behind the wall of monitors.

For the first time, I notice a space behind the green screen panel. There, Mom has dragged a dozen monoliths into a rough circle. I pull open the access panel for the closest one and plug in the enhancer. The more I stare at these monolith towers, the more I wonder.

"Who's coming to help?" I ask. "I mean, I know it's someone from a different world in a parallel dimension, but that's not very specific." It could be a creature made from Jell-O for all I know.

Jell-O would be cool, actually.

Mom keeps typing at a frantic pace. "A man."

"Anything interesting? Scales? Extra eyes?"

"Really. You and your imagination." Mom shakes her head. "It will be a large, older, and somewhat angry man with a slight disfigurement. His name is Cole."

I turn the name over in my head. *Cole.* It feels familiar, like something from one of my dreams. Then again, that happens to me a lot.

Mom continues. "Cole is powerful enough that he can get Luci out of any difficulty." She purses her lips as she types even faster. "Your sister may be involved in things even your friend the Scythe could never handle."

All of a sudden, it's make sense why Mom would waited for the chance to bringing in this level of help. On some level, it's comforting that she's had a plan this long, even if she couldn't communicate it.

Mom types a few last lines and hits the *Enter* key. "And here we go!"

My pulse speeds. Lights blink on in the monoliths towers. The lab floor vibrates softly as a low hum fills the air. Mom clicks a few more keystrokes. "Do you see anything?"

A moment later, something changes in the center of floor between the monoliths. The old tile gleams like it's made of glass. After that, it cracks. The effect looks like someone's trying to punch their way through the floor from below. *Perfect*. The drift void is beginning, and there's a formal name for this stage of its development.

"We have spiral frac," I announce.

"Excellent. How large is the instance?"

"Filling up the entire floor between the monoliths." In other words, larger than any spiral frac in recorded science. But the final drift void will need to be big if we want to hit a parallel universe. Current drift voids have only connected to remote parts of the same building. No one's gone beyond that yet.

"Upping the power levels." More clicks sounds from Mom's keyboard.

The low hum intensifies. Small lights on the monoliths shine more brightly. The faint scent of ozone fills the air. The glass-like fractures on the floor begin to melt.

After that, they spin.

Between the monoliths, the floor's checkerboard pattern transforms. The black and white tiles merge and swirl, reminding me of white paint being mixed into its black counterpart. I smile. The next stage is here.

"We've got an active vortex," I announce.

When Mom speaks again, there's no hiding the excitement in her voice. "More power coming your way." There's an ominous single click as she hits the *Enter* key.

The monoliths flare with even more energy. The low hum from these devices accelerates into a high-pitched mechanical screech. From the small lights on each monolith, thin beams of brightness cut through the air. The floor shakes more violently; the scent of ozone grows stronger.

The active vortex darkens. The swirl of energy accelerates until the floor collapses in on itself. What looks like a churning black hole descends, its depths partially illuminated by flickering lights from the monoliths.

The moment burns into my memory. Mom and I just created the largest drift void in history. A mixture of awe and joy zing through my nervous system.

It's overwhelming.

Beautiful.

And most of all, dangerous.

My limbs tremble with excitement. "It's here," I announce. There's no need to say what has arrived. *The drift void*.

"I've never seen one appear so quickly," says Mom.

With those words, everything goes berserk.

Bolts of lightning shoot up from the drift void. My breath catches. How does anything escape a black hole? Then I remember. This isn't a black hole. It's a drift void. No one knows what properties it has in general, let alone at this size.

Better move quickly.

I cup my hand by my mouth. "Toss me the brush."

Mom fiddles with the pocket on her lab coat. She only takes a moment, but the action seems to last for hours. At last, Mom pulls free the brush with Luci's hair and tosses it toward me. Catching it, I quickly pull free a single white-blond strand.

A wall of fire erupts from the drift void. It's both searingly hot and pitch dark in color.

Black fire. Did not see that coming.

I take a half step backward. The white bolts of lighting dance within the black fire. My breath catches. Whatever is happening here, I know two things.

One, it isn't good.

Two, it's getting worse.

I drop the lone blonde strand into the vortex. The black flame warms my skin, but it doesn't burn. The moment Luci's hair enters the drift void, all signs of fire and lightning instantly disappear.

A weight of worry seeps from my shoulders. The drift void no longer appears dangerous, and it's accepted Luci's DNA.

"It's in," I call.

"Good," says Mom. "I'll just shut down—"

Before Mom can finish, a fresh plume of black fire erupts from the drift void. This time, the flames lick against the ceiling. More lighting than ever before blasts through the dark fire. I fall backward onto my butt.

"Mom! Off! Now!"

When my mother speaks again, her voice has a frantic edge. "The system's not responding."

Across the entire lab, every monolith shakes and screeches. Beams of brightness slice out from all the tower seams. The monoliths look ready to burst, and not just the ones encircling the drift void. Every tower in the lab goes berserk. Waves of dark fire erupt, expanding out across the lab floor. My thoughts condense to one concept.

Save Mom.

I race over to my mother. Pulling Mom's frail body to the floor, I cover her frame with my own. Black flames roll across us. Like before, the fire sears but doesn't burn. Lightning strikes the lab from floor to ceiling. The monoliths rattle so violently, it's clear they have only seconds before they burst apart.

"Mom, where are the power breakers?" I ask. Those are a series of switches that channel energy for the lab. I need to shut them off and fast. That's the only way to stop the drift void.

"Far corner," she replies.

Through the fire and smoke, I can make out the small gray metal box attached to the wall.

That's it. The power breakers.

I rise up and take one step closer. Two. Flames erupt round me. Lighting bolts strike the floor nearby, tearing huge holes in the tiles.

Then it ends.

Perfect stillness follows.

No fire.

No lightning.

No sound.

Around us, the view of the lab turns into a series of what look like photographs. Left, right, front, back. I turn around but can no longer see anything but the dualities of things. My insides freeze over with shock as I realize what's happening.

Everything is two-dimensional.

We've slipped into a different level of space-time.

This will definitely show up on Authority's tracking systems. Based on how the government scans energy, this might even look like a nuclear blast went off in western Mass. No question what to do next.

Shut it all down.

"Stay put," I call to Mom.

Stepping forward, I'm careful to keep on a direct route to the power breakers. There are no 360-degree views in two-dimensional space-time. If I deviate from this razor-thin path, I'll lock onto another view ... and lose all sight of my goal.

I can't let that happen.

With careful movements, I march closer to the circuit breaker.

Ten feet away.

Five.

At last, the small metal box is before me. Whipping it open, I shut down every switch inside.

Life returns to three dimensions.

With it, there comes fire and lightning.

A final plume of black flame engulfs the laboratory. All the monoliths explode with bursts of sparks. Bits of metal and plastic rain down on the floor. The scent of burned oil fills the air. I crouch down, cover my head, and flat-out panic.

What made me think this was a good idea?

A second later, the drift void vanishes. The monoliths stand as charred-out ruins. Smoke coils up from their blasted interiors. Broken glass vials litter the floor. I race back to Mom.

"Are you all right?"

Her blue eyes shine with pure joy. "Isn't it exciting? We're the first ones to visit the second dimension!"

"Yeah, it's ... great."

"What's wrong?"

I wave her off. "Nothing. Just the shock of discovery."

"You'll get used to it. You're brilliant."

Normally, I'd soak in that praise. This time, my thoughts race to a different place. The more I think about it, the more I'm certain the government will see this as a nuclear blast. They'll follow up by checking the live satellite feed for this area. That will confirm there are no mushroom cloud or leveled buildings. At that point, the Authority should conclude it's a system glitch. At least, that's what they did ten years ago when a software upgrade gave them the same misread. If they follow a similar process, then a patrol will be sent to investigate within twenty-four hours.

I rake my fingers through my hair. But things have changed since ten years ago. Now the Lacerator has started hanging out in this area. Maybe the government will connect the dots and send in a patrol much faster. I tap my cheek and think things through. Bottom line? I give the Merciless two hours before they show up at our door. A science crime this big means we'll be executed.

I need to make any sign of this disappear.

Damn. It's time to ask Fritz for help. Again.

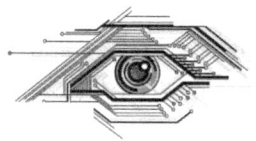

CHAPTER 13

MOM and I just slipped into the second dimension. It's exhilarating and terrifying.

Who am I kidding? It's mostly terrifying.

I check my smart watch. 8:00 am. There's no time to find a secure spot to chat with Fritz. I glance over at Mom. She stands stock still, looking out over the ruined lab. If I chat with hologram-Fritz here, she'll be fine. Mom doesn't like that I work for the Scythe, but she won't stop me, either.

Lifting my wrist, I type my emergency code into my smart watch. *Come on, Fritz.* I hit the dial button. Instantly, an alert flashes on the small screen.

CALLS BLOCKED.

I can't say this is a surprise. It's not like Fritz didn't warn me that he was done using phone comms. Even so, I have other options. Using the tiny screen keypad, I send a text message to *Happy Time Cleaning*—that's Fritz's cover business.

Freelance 11 to HappyTimeCleaning: Need to talk. I have another emergency.

I stare at my smart watch like it's Fritz's face before me. All my emotion and focus pours into that little screen. At last, more text appears.

TYPING REPLY ...

My shoulders loosen. Fritz is still taking my texts. *This is good.* All I need to do is get him to receive my hologram call. After that, we can fix this entire disaster. Fritz's reply appears on the miniature screen.

HappyTimeCleaning to Freelance11: We talk face to face ONLY.

My insides twist with worry. That's not the response I was hoping for. I peck out a quick response.

Freelance11 to HappyTimeCleaning: Please. I'm desperate.

This time, there's no sign Fritz is writing a reply. Instead, another alert flashes on the watch face.

MESSAGES BLOCKED.

I stifle the urge to groan. Fritz won't even take my texts. That means I have to haul my butt over to the Scythe's lair, which is on the other side of Winter's Run. If I race at full speed, I can get there in twenty minutes, tops. After that, I can cut another deal. Maybe Fritz wants a second magnetic enhancer.

Beside me, Mom wavers where she stands. "We've done well, Meimi. If Cole can help us, he'll arrive soon." A faraway look returns to her eyes. "Let's head to the kitchen. Miss Edith should be here already."

I wrap my arm around my mother's shoulder. Her body feels so wispy next to mine. Already, her eyes are taking on that glazed look I know so well. Suddenly, I wish I'd asked her a million questions while she was clear-headed. Why does Mom feel so guilty about the lab accident with Dad? Are there any pictures of my father hidden somewhere? How did Mom find out Luci is still alive? Instead, Mom and I spent our time opening a drift void and flipping the factory into the second dimension.

Was it worth it?

I tilt my head, considering. *Oh, yeah. That was totally worth it.*

Working the drift with Mom is the best, pure and simple. Even if it does bring the Merciless down on our heads.

Helping to bolster Mom, I walk us both out of the laboratory and toward the kitchen. I'll be honest. Some not-too-small part of me would love to leave right now, but when Mom's like this, there's no way she'll get back safely on her own. Once I get her settled, I can rush off and meet Fritz.

We begin what should be a short walk to the front of the factory. The scientist part of my head knows that we're moving along at a fairly good pace. Even so, it feels like it takes hours to shuffle our way across the factory floor. In my head, every tall vat of chemicals looms large as a mountain in our path. Each knot of pipes seems to tangle around our ankles like pricker vines.

Finally, we get close enough to the kitchen that I see Miss Edith through the opened door. She raises a chipped teacup in motion that I've seen so many times before. Without saying a word, she's asking: *do you want any?*

I call across the factory floor. "No tea for me this morning, Miss Edith."

"It's not for you," she counters.

"Mom doesn't want any either." I don't need to ask my mother her opinion on this; Mom never drinks tea.

Finally, I guide Mom back to the kitchen door. Then I freeze.

"The tea is for your guest, Meimi." After that, Miss Edith hands the cup to a young guy who leans against the countertop. He's wearing black body armor.

Smiling, he takes the cup from Miss Edith's hands. "Thank you."

Beside me, Mom grips my hand so tightly, I'm sure she'll leave a bruise.

"This is it," Mom whispers. "He's here. This is the visitor who'll help us."

In other words, here's our alien.

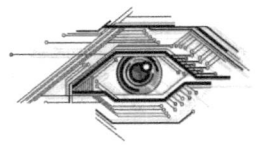

CHAPTER 14

*W*AIT, *WHAT?*

I blink extra-fast, not believing what I'm seeing. Then I scan the kitchen again.

The guy in black body armor is still there.

He looks about eighteen, tall and strong with military-style hair, a square jawline, and soulful blue eyes. Scientifically speaking, he's handsome.

And familiar.

Where have I seem him before?

Our gazes lock. Parts of my soul twist. Energies shift. Connections form. I must be under major stress again, because I'm having that same illusion I did before with the Lacerator. A thin haze of blue particles forms around me. Mom and Miss Edith don't seem to notice anything, but I swear, the boy catches the change right away.

Emptions whirl through me.

Once again, they aren't mine.

Without knowing how, I'm certain these feelings come from this boy.

There's the prickle of surprise.

A chill of awe.

The heat of desire.

My muscles freeze. How can this boy be feeling all these things about me? We don't even know each other. Again, as with the Lacerator, images flicker through my mind. Last time, the Lacerator sent me pictures as a means of communication. This time, they aren't pictures as much as rich experiences. I don't know where these mental videos are coming from, just that they flash from one scene to the next.

Flash. It's nighttime. This boy and I ride hoverbikes side by side high over a strange city. Lights blink beneath us. We're laughing.

Flash. He and I stand on a sandy landscape. Both of us hold swords. We're back to back and ready for battle.

Flash. It's an empty dance floor. An orchestra plays a slow tune. The boy wears a tuxedo; I'm in a black dress. We dance slowly, our arms wounds around each other, my head resting on his shoulder.

Before, what the Lacerator sent me were like fancy hieroglyphs—more an attempt at communication that anything else. Now, what I'm experiencing feels different.

Detailed.

Moving.

Real.

Shaking my head, I break the connection. The mist of blue particles disappears. This proves it. I have been under way too much stress lately. If I thought what happened with the Lacerator was bad, this is an entirely new level of stress-induced hallucination.

I actively ignore the little voice in my head that pleads this could also be real.

Whatever it is, I have bigger priorities. I simply must finalize this deal with Fritz.

Careful to avoid looking in the boy's direction, I walk Mom over to her favorite chair. She slips into place. "Thank you so much for coming," she says. "You look just like Cole."

"He's my father." The boy stands and bows slightly in Mom's direction. "Thorne Oxblood, at your service."

Every nerve ending in my body goes on alert. That voice. The name. *Thorne.* It can't be from my dreams, can it? Scanning my memories, I try to recall what else happened in those night visions. There was something about an omniverse. Other than that, the whole thing is a blur.

Stupid dreams.

Miss Edith takes another sip from her tea sup. "I like this one," she says. "You can ignore that MacGregor boy."

Thorne arches his brows. "MacGregor?"

"It's nothing," I say quickly. "Thanks for the tip, Miss Edith."

After everything else that happened this morning, comments from Miss Edith shouldn't make me blush. After all, who cares that this is a hot alien boy and Miss Edith is mentioning some guy I fake-married in second grade?

Even so, my face burns up about six different shades of red.

Stupid face.

Mom presses her forehead against the windowpane by her chair. When she next speaks, she doesn't look in Thorne's direction. "Can you help us?"

My heart sinks. Mom's voice has returned to a hollow murmur. The lab maven from this morning is gone.

I take a half step backward, trying to take this all in. Mom made a deal with some huge, scarred-up guy named Cole from another world. And now his scientifically handsome son, Thorne, is here to make good on everything while triggering vague memories from my dreams. And I had a mind-meld experience with him for some reason, too. Let's not forget that little side order of strangeness.

If I didn't need to haul my butt to the Scythe, I'd have a lot of Meimi-style questions for this situation.

Thorne nods. "I can make good on your pact with my father." He turns to me. When he next speaks, his voice holds a tone that can only be called reverent. "And you are?"

His gaze locks with mine again. All I can think about was that connection we just had. Those visions felt so deep and real. What's going on here?

I guess a long pause went by without my speaking, because Miss Edith answers for me. "She's Meimi Archer, and Rose here is her mother. I'm the hired help. More tea?"

"No, thank you," intones Thorne.

"Such a sweet boy." Miss Edith turns to me. "But you should watch those security systems of yours. He walked right into this building."

Which raises a good question. I focus on Miss Edith. "You didn't notice anything about the building when you came in?" Like the fact that it flipped in space-time, not that I say that part out loud.

"No, should I have?" she asks.

I shrug. "Just making conversation. And you're right—I'll look into the security systems. In the meantime, can you please get Mom a blanket?"

Miss Edith takes another sip from her teacup. "She doesn't look cold."

"Mom and I need a moment alone with Thorne."

"Ah, I understand." Miss Edith glances at Mom who's taken to staring out the window again. Miss Edith wags her finger at me. "No funny business while I'm gone."

"Meaning?" I ask.

Miss Edith lifts her chin. "No kissing."

I pinch the bridge of my nose. *Like I'd make out with some random guy while my catatonic mother is nearby.* Or anywhere, really.

"Thank you, Miss Edith. I'll remember that."

Miss Edith leaves, doing one of those old lady hums as she goes. I swear, this is probably the most excitement she's had in years.

Once Miss Edith is gone and out of earshot, I risk a quick glance at Thorne. "Mom called you here to find my sister Luci."

Thorne nods slowly. "She's the DNA sample you sent."

"Can you find lost humans ... I mean missing, uh, people ... Earthlings?" I press my lips together, hard. This makes the catastrophe conversation with G look like I was Miss Suave.

Stop talking, Meimi.

A small smile rounds his full lips. Not that I find his mouth attractive or anything. This is just a scientific comment on the ratio of mouth to face. "I can do all sorts of things. Let me demonstrate."

When I first saw Thorne, he was wearing heavy black body armor. Now, that covering starts to shimmer with a violet-colored glow. The structure changes until Thorne no longer wears body armor at all. Instead, his outfit morphs into dark jeans, a black Henley, and heavy boots. Thorne gestures across his torso.

"I have synthetic and organic micro-machines that are merged with my nervous system. We call them the Sentient. With their help, I can create armor, tap into computer systems, and even break through some kinds of walls. I will find your sister."

The Sentient ... something about that feels familiar, but the whole *getting murdered by the Authority* thing has me a little distracted.

Thorne focuses his big blue eyes on me, breaking me out of my thoughts. "I'll start looking for your sister once I set up some additional systems."

"Do you need any equipment? My lab is downstairs and I have some gear there."

"Thank you. That would be very helpful. While I'm at it, Miss Edith brought up a good point. I suggest some security enhancements to the factory. I can link in some of my Sentient to the system and track intruders more efficiently." He stares sheepishly at his feet. "I don't have many Sentient, but the ones I have are effective."

"I'm sure they're amazing." I rub my neck and think things through. This guy can conjure miniature robot things. If he were going to hurt me or Mom, he would have done it by now. "Any security upgrades you can make would be great."

Miss Edith blusters back into the room, bringing Mom a blanket. She gives me and Thorne a knowing stare. "You two look cozy." She then mouths the words: *keep saving yourself for this one.*

A jolt of shock moves across my skin. Was my virginity just broadcast across the kitchen?

I look to Thorne. His biting his lips together, hard.

Why, yes. Yes, it was.

It's beyond time to leave. "Oh, wow. Just got a message from my smart watch."

Miss Edith sips her tea and grins. "I didn't hear any beeps. Doesn't your watch ding when you get an alert?"

It does, which brings up two facts. One, Miss Edith is a total gear-head, which I already knew. Two, I really need to leave before she does something else that's supremely embarrassing.

"I'll just take off for school now." Even saying the word *school* sends fresh waves of adrenaline churning through me. School isn't my real destination. It's Fritz. That'll be tons of not-fun.

All the color seems to drain from Thorne's face. "You're going to school alone? Where are your guards?"

"Guards? This is a Learning Squirrel High School. The only thing you need to guard me from is our science teacher, the Bummer." I make little quotation marks with my fingers when I say *the Bummer*. Thorne doesn't find it amusing, though. If anything, the look on his face turns more intense.

"Guards," he repeats.

Scooping up my backpack from the floor, I open my backpack and show him the interior. "Weapons," I counter.

Miss Edith totters over to stand beside me. "Are those chem darts? Can I play with them?"

Like I said, Miss Edith is a gearhead.

"Sure you can," I say to Miss Edith. "But later." As in a lot later.

I refocus on Thorne. By the way, it's really great that we aren't having any more mind connection incidents. That definitely supports the theory that I've been having a series of mini nervous breakdowns.

A little sad that I'm pulling for the breakdown option here, but I am.

"Are we good?" I ask Thorne.

"For now." The way he says those words, it's as if I should attend school with a team of bazooka-wielding guards ... and he'll make sure that happens and soon.

"See you," I call. Hoisting up my backpack, I make a beeline for the door. Thorne doesn't follow me. I decide that's a good thing.

Fritz doesn't play well with others.

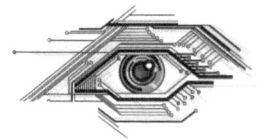

CHAPTER 15

IT DOESN'T TAKE LONG to reach the Scythe's secret lair. After I hit the outskirts of Winter's Run, I shimmy up an old drainage ditch. After that, I scramble through old water pipes for a bit. The access pipeline is round, about five feet tall, and lined with rust. The stale scent of mold hangs in the air. After a few feet, a horse fly hovers nearby, its body gleaming with a metallic sheen. I should have guessed this was coming.

It's another one of Fritz's drones.

He already knows I'm here.

Finally, I reach a portal door in the wall. *The entrance to Scythe central.* I knock on the thick metal and wave at the drone. That's all the greeting I'm giving.

Fritz pulls open the portal a crack. A slice of his pale face is visible. "You vant something, Meimi?"

What do I want? How about we skip the fake German accent? Sadly, there isn't time today for our usual banter.

"You know I've got a situation, Fritz. Let me in."

"Ya, ya, vee help." Fritz pulls open the door, revealing a concrete chamber with a low ceiling. Wooden benches line the floor. People are waiting everywhere, all of them miserable. There's a guy in rags shaking for his next fix. An older woman with a young girl on her lap. Some folks even wear office worker uniforms with the insignia of the Authority on their chests.

Fritz opens a metal door lining the opposite wall. I follow. Together, we enter a refurbished utility closet that serves as Fritz's office. It fits a small desk, a set of wobbly chairs, and not much else. I sit and wait until

Fritz positions his massive bulk behind the tiny table. Once he's in place, my not-a-father focuses on me.

"What's your emergency *this time*?" All trace of the fake German accent is gone.

"I set off some government alarms."

Fritz glances at his tabletop, which is one huge touch monitor. "According to these government data feeds, a supposed nuclear blast went off in western Mass ... without actually going off. They think it's a glitch, but Merciless are still being deployed to this area for arrival at 9 am. It's now 8:40 am. Is this you?"

"Mom and I worked the drift this morning." I pause, waiting for Fritz to be impressed that Mom was lucid. Instead, the tips of his ears turn red.

Whoa. Fritz is really enraged.

"Here's what happened," I say. "The Ozymandias factory slipped into two-dimensional space-time for a little while. It's showing up as a nuclear blast to the Authority because no one's gone 2-D before."

"I don't like Merciless crawling all over my part of the state, Meimi. The Scythe pays big money to stay off grid."

"I'm sorry. Mom wanted to work the drift and—" I stop myself before saying anything about aliens or finding Luci. "—I guess we got caught up. Please clean things up for me, like you did with RCM1."

Muscles flicker along Fritz's thick neck. "Not so easy this time, Meims. You're coming to me with a major science crime and all of twenty minutes to cover it up." He narrows his eyes. "And all because you flipped an entire factory into two dimensional space-time." Fritz presses some buttons on the top of his desk. "Did you hear that, boss?"

My stomach seems to tumble through the floor. *Fritz has been transmitting our conversation to the Scythe.*

A crackle sounds over the intercom. A deep, silky voice fills the small room. "Bring her in." I'd know that tone anywhere.

The Scythe.

Fritz slumps forward. If I didn't know the guy was incapable of feeling, I'd think he was relieved.

Shivering, Fritz exhales a long breath.

My eyes widen with surprise. I take it back. Fritz is definitely relieved. That's a good sign. The Scythe must at least be interested in helping to cover things up for me. If it weren't an option, then I'd just be chucked out on to the street. Or worse, terminated. Even so, I'm curious what possible deal would interest the Scythe enough to save me. Hopefully, another magnetic enhancer will do the trick.

I give Fritz my most innocent look. This has about a fifty percent success ratio in getting him to spill his guts. "The Scythe wants to see me?" I ask.

I've met the Scythe once before, when I first started doing freelance work for his organization. All I remember about him is that he's tall, dark, handsome, and—most of all—scary as hell.

I blink some more. It can't hurt. "Do you know what he wants?"

"Nice try," deadpans Fritz. "I'm telling you zero. Come along, there's no getting around it now." He whips open a drawer in his desk and pulls out a black sack with a flourish. "You know the rules. Put this on."

I slip the hood over my head. It blocks out any view of the outside world and smells like bad breath and cigarette smoke. Fritz leads me around for about ten minutes or so. All the while, my heart pounds against my rib cage.

Eventually, his heavy hands press on my shoulders. "Sit."

I plunk down onto the softest leather seat that my backside ever touched.

There's the clink of ice cubes in a glass, followed by a low chuckle. I know those noises. The Scythe is perpetually holding a glass of whiskey. And that laugh? It's smooth as silk and terrifying as lightning.

"You can remove the hood," says the Scythe.

Fritz pulls the cloth from my head. I find myself sitting in a posh office, like something you see in contraband magazines from before the Authority, like *Beautiful Life* or *United We Stand*. Plus, everything in here is sleek black and stainless steel. There's a wide desk, and behind that desk sits Mister Tall, Dark, and Terrifying. It's his eyes, I decide. There's no emotion in them.

"Leave us, Fritz," intones the Scythe.

"Yes, sir."

I sense more than see Fritz depart from the room. A long pause follows where I get another look at my employer. His dark suit is well tailored and paired with a matching shirt and indigo tie. Dark scruff lines his chin, and his short-ish black hair is perfectly coiffed.

The Scythe takes a long sip of whiskey. "You've gotten yourself into a spot of trouble, Meimi Archer. Worse than RCM1, even. And that was rather something."

"Please, you must stop the Merciless from getting to my home. Mom and Miss Edith are there. Plus—" I stop myself before adding Thorne to the list. "It was just a little slip-up, really."

"Shifting an entire factory into two-dimensional space-time is more than a slip-up. That's a major science crime."

My palms turn slick with sweat. "But you can hide it, right?"

"Yes, I have contacts who can bury this for me. Everyone owes me favors. But I need something very specific in return."

"I can make another magnetic enhancer. You can have it. Free."

"No, I need something else. An invention specifically for working the drift. You must have heard the government is in need of fresh science skills."

"There was something about this at school. Doctor Godwin says they need experts in chemistry, mechanics, and drift science."

"Have *you* ever thought of getting a sponsor and attending ECHO Academy?"

I frown. *Where is he going with this?*

"No," I state.

"Really? I could be that sponsor, you know."

Ah, so that's where he's going.

Two words on that particular concept: *fat chance.*

"Look," I begin. "Things are fine between us, just how they are. I can walk away. You can, too. I've heard about those sponsorship contracts. You get a so-called free education, but then you spend the rest of your life paying back those loans. I'm not signing some contract to be owned by *anyone* for a lifetime."

A long pause follows as the Scythe sips his drink and eyes me carefully. At length, he speaks again. "No, I don't think you would. Not willingly, in any case. And there are limits to what even I can do."

His words make the small hairs on my neck stand on end. "Not sure what you mean."

"I refer to the ECHO Academy, that's all. You're right, the Authority needs help in terms of chemistry, mechanics, and drift science. Again, that last category—drift science—is proving especially tricky. The Authority can't find talent."

"I'm guessing they can't blast knowledge into people's heads either. Well, not without turning them into the equivalent of mental cabbage."

"True."

I sit up straighter in my chair. "I won't work for the Authority."

"I've sold your inventions to the government before."

"And how much has that helped them? Zero. I put fail safes on stuff so my work can't be reverse engineered."

"In that case, we should continue things the way they've been going, shouldn't we?" asks the Scythe. "The magnetic enhancer you created for me; that was a rather impressive invention. The Authority knows I have a freelance agent who can do the impossible with ease. They need skills like yours. As a result, they are willing to pay me very well. That means you'll benefit, too. Interested?"

"As long as I can put in my fail safes, I'm fine." *Especially if it keeps me and Mom alive.*

"I can talk the Authority off this morning's science crime, but my guess is that they'll want something in return. Fortunately, I've already been in discussions regarding our next project."

"What kind of project?"

"One that will prove to the Authority that my freelancer is just what they need, alive." He slides a data pad across his desk. "Take a look."

Picking up the device, I scan the schematics displayed on screen. "They want something that creates drift voids." I shake my head. "You do realize there are already plenty of labs that can do this already? All you need are a bunch of monoliths."

"Read on."

So I do just that. A moment later, my heart sinks. "They want something that's small enough to fit in a briefcase and it's aimed at my school? Why my school?"

The Scythe holds his whiskey up to the light. "That was my addition. I was feeling rather mischievous after all this extra effort you've been putting me through. You see, I do so love listening to all your conversations with Fritz. I knew you'd give him trouble over the location."

"Listening in on other people's conversations is a violation of privacy."

The Scythe pauses from examining his whiskey to give me a dry look. "I care."

In a way, the Scythe has a point. There are bigger things to worry about now than how the Scythe is a creeper who listens in on me and Fritz. Leaning back in my chair, I think through this latest project.

"What do you say?" asks the Scythe. "Can you create this?"

"Creating that large of a void over my school could erase the whole building. The structure could get sent to another universe or dimension, even."

"I notice you didn't say it was impossible, just impractical." He grins. "Feel free to edit the specifications so the device works in the middle of the night when no one's around. Put in as many fail safes as you want. And continue reading until the end."

I scan the final set of specs and shiver. "You want this done by midnight *tonight?*"

"All I require is a working prototype. Make it solid enough for one use, if you prefer. But I do need to prove to my contacts that you're the real deal. Quickly."

I rake my hands through my hair and think things through. This is crazy. Huge drift voids on demand? I can do it, but I'd have to repurpose a bunch of stuff in my lab. That won't be easy. "How small does the prototype need to be? Are we talking a big briefcase maybe?"

"One that fits in this." The Scythe sets a sleek black briefcase onto his tabletop. "And only this."

"So, it needs to go in a super-small case. That's not possible."

"You always say that to Fritz, and then you always deliver."

Something in his tone makes my blood boil. "I could just find my own buyers, you know."

The Scythe chuckles again. "Once the Merciless tear through your home, you and your family won't be breathing, let alone able to reach out to alternate buyers." He finishes his drink and sets down the empty glass. "Face it. You need me far more than I need you."

My spine stiffens. "You'll double cross me."

"And miss out on my ongoing paycheck from your services? Have you learned nothing about me after all these years?" The Scythe leans forward in his chair. "One minute remains before 9 a.m., Meimi. Do I call my contacts, or do you *try* to run?"

I've heard people talk about their heads spinning, but I literally feel like my brain is on a Tilt-A-Whirl. I press my palms onto my temples, hoping I can squeeze some clear thoughts into my skull.

All I can think is that I have thirty seconds left.

"All right," I say quickly. "You'll have the prototype by midnight." *Maybe.*

"Excellent." The Scythe taps a few buttons on his desktop. "Fritz, cover things up for Meimi."

Fritz's familiar voice echoes into the room. "Yes, sir."

"Glad we could come to an arrangement," declares the Scythe. "I'll send Fritz to pick up the prototype from your home at midnight. You can keep the data pad and specifications. My gift."

I slip the device into my backpack. "We didn't discuss something. How much will you pay me?"

"Ah, we didn't cover that topic, now did we?" The Scythe gives me one of those looks where he could shoot me dead and not care one bit. "Why, your payment is that you and your family stay alive."

"That's not fair."

"I'm not Fritz. This isn't up for discussion." The Scythe gestures toward the door. "If you don't mind, I have some calls to make in order to assist Fritz. There are some members of the Authority who will be very pleased to learn their bank accounts have miraculously increased, in exchange for wiping your science crime away."

"I'll leave you to it." I don't wait for more chatter. After grabbing the briefcase, I haul my butt toward the exit. With every step, the same question keeps repeating through my mind.

Am I doing the right thing? And why would anyone want small equipment to build large drift voids on demand?

In the end, I decide there's no point in worrying. Whatever the reason, building this prototype is the only way to keep me and Mom alive. When it comes to creating the device, I'll put safeguards on my safeguards. No one will be able to use it twice or figure out how I put the thing together.

At least, I hope not.

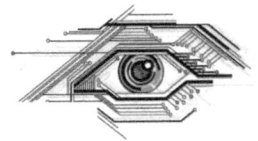

CHAPTER 16

THE MOMENT I step outside the Scythe's door, Fritz sets another sack over my head. I don't gasp or put up a fight. Why bother? *Get me out of here already.* In no time, I'm back outside the drainpipe and hoofing it toward home.

As I race along, I plan how to build the prototype. Computer code flickers through my thoughts. Next I see different components from my lab lining up inside the briefcase. Pieces of wire mentally snap into place around them, along with a host of brackets, sensors, and data chips.

I can do this.

By the time I reach my door, some kind of greenish drizzle has started to fall. I lift up the metal flap that covers my security pad and freeze.

Someone's upgraded our security system. There are no more codes to enter. Instead there's a pad for placing my hand to confirm identity. There's even a retinal scanner installed as a double layer of security.

My heart jumps into my throat. This enhanced security system makes me feel less safe than ever before. Mostly because I didn't build it. But I know who did.

Thorne.

I suppose that should make me feel a little better. After all, Thorne did ask if he could make the enhancements. It doesn't, though. This is major tech that he installed in under an hour. Even if I had all the parts handy, this project would take days. And didn't he say something about integrating his Sentient as well? Who is this guy? I mean, beyond the obvious alien thing.

Whoever he is, standing out in an acid rainstorm won't help.

I set my palm against the scanner. Green lights flicker—both across my palm and into my eyes—before a smooth feminine voice speaks.

"Welcome home, Meimi." With that, the door opens automatically.

Wow. A new security system that even talks. This really should be a good thing. So why have I broken out in a sweat?

Rushing inside, I make my way to the kitchen. Mom sits at her favorite chair, staring out the window. Miss Edith stands at our stove, heating up another pot of tea. She looks up as I approach. "Meimi."

"Hey, Miss Edith. How's Mom?"

"Same as always." She purses her lined mouth. "You're home early."

"We only had a half day today at school in order to...uh..."

"What, dear?"

I'm a scientist, not a professional liar. "To celebrate President Hope's birthday."

"That was last month."

"Well, we're still celebrating." I stalk around the kitchen, scanning for more signs of security upgrades. "Everything okay in here?"

"Both your mother and I are fine."

"So who changed the security system?"

"It was that nice young man, Thorne. He's rather handy."

A fluttery feeling takes up resident in my chest. "Where is he?" I ask.

"Down in your workroom."

"Oh." For some reason, that's all I can get out.

"Why don't you go say hello?" She lowers her voice. "I think he fancies you."

"Why? What did he say?" I hate the desperate edge to my voice. I don't care about some handsome guy who enhances security systems. And who's also an alien that maybe I had a telepathic connection with.

Ugh, my life is strange.

"He said something about helping you," adds Miss Edith.

"Right. I'll just go to my workroom now, I guess."

So that's what I do. But with every step, my limbs shiver with a crazy mix of fear and excitement.

I'm about to see Thorne again.

Minutes later, I push open the heavy metal door to our basement. Inside, my lab is a mess of wires, computer parts, and souped-up monoliths. Before, I'd thought my place would be pretty sad compared to what I imagined was inside Mom's lab. Now, I can appreciate my workroom for the little slice of awesome that it is.

Sure enough, Thorne is here and waist-deep into one of my monoliths. The guy doesn't even look up as I approach. It gives me a chance to appreciate the play of muscle on his legs.

Scientifically speaking, the guy is ripped.

"Hi, there," I say.

No reply.

Thorne might not be acting rude, though. After all, the guy's head is deep inside a monolith, so there's that.

"How's it going?" I ask, my voice louder.

Thorne's attention stays focused on something inside the monolith. "Slowly. Your systems need a ton of upgrades. There's not much I can do without the right gear."

I twist my fingers together at my waist. "Look, maybe I should have said this before, but I was a little distracted. You should know that Mom and I flipped this factory into two-dimensional space-time. Now our government may be sending over soldiers to pick up everyone. Although I hope they don't because I just made a deal with a criminal overlord named the Scythe to prevent that."

Thorne stops fiddling around inside the monolith. Leaning out, he looks up at me. The boy's all square jaw, brush-cut hair, and intense blue eyes. The connection we had in the kitchen comes back again. I don't need to look down to see I have blue particles around me again. Emotions stream through my heart. This time, all of them come from Thorne.

A fire of protective rage.

Electric jolts of affection.

The chill of determination.

The sensations are overpowering. For a moment, I forget that they are all probably figments of my imagination. Words tumble from my mouth. "These feelings..." I stammer. "What do they mean?"

"That I don't care who's coming or what the risks are. I won't leave you, Meimi."

I suck in a shocked breath. The motion severs the ties with the particles. All of them disappear. I choose to ignore how comfortable I'm getting with this mind-meld thing. Part of me is still pulling for the mental breakdown option.

Thorne rises. "You're mine to protect."

"Why would you say that? You don't know me."

His gaze locks with mine. "The past, present, and future are all constructs. In some dimensions, they all exist at the same moment."

I nod. "Sure, that's one of the first things you learn in drift science."

"In many of these other places and dimensions, you and I already know each other. In fact, our connection is so strong, it's bleeding over into this reality. My people call it *finding your transcendent*. It's incredibly rare. Not to mention, unexpected." He gives me a sad smile. "Especially for me."

So I'm this guy's transcendent? My head fogs over with memory. Did I dream about transcendents? I push to recall. Sadly, no matter how hard I press, I can't remember anything else. There are more traditional ways to get answers, though.

"Something happened between us in the kitchen," I begin. "Is that true, or am I having some kind of hallucination?"

"It's true." He steps closer. "It happened."

Images pop into my mind. RCM1. Godwin. The Lacerator. "This isn't the first time it's happened. The Authority—that's our government—has this genetically enhanced attack animal called the Lacerator. Not an animal exactly; it's more like a particle monster." I huff out a breath. "This is so hard to explain."

"Did it look like this?" On Thorne's arm, his Henley changes back into body armor. "Now, I'll slow the process down."

Sure enough, once the transformation moves more slowly, I can clearly see the tiny particles that hover over his skin as they realign into a new shape.

"Definitely. That's what the Lacerator looked like."

"That wasn't a monster. It's what I was telling you about before. The Sentient. Most exist in a swarm. Most likely, this Lacerator of yours is an independent cyber swarm." He moves even nearer, stopping when his body warmth seeps into mine. "If they are interested, a swarm can choose to link to people for short periods of time."

I blink hard, trying to process this news. "So all that was real." All of a sudden, my legs feel wobbly beneath me.

"This is a lot of information," says Thorne gently. "We can discuss it another time. I don't wish to overwhelm you."

"No, I can do this." Some small part of my mind says my dreams have been preparing me for this moment, but I'm too focused on Thorne's to consider much else.

"Tell me. What happened when you encountered the Lacerator?"

"I could feel its emotions. Images also appeared in my mind. It was some way of communicating with me. But with you, it was different. I got these crazy visions of us doing things together."

"My poor Meimi. You must have so many questions."

"I do, but I'm also in trouble. If you can find Luci and manipulate the Sentient, maybe you can help with this." I zip open my backpack, pull out the Scythe's data pad, and hand it over to Thorne. "I told you I made a deal before. Here's what it is. If I can build this by midnight, then the Merciless won't attack my home. Can you help me?"

Thorne stares at the walls. "You don't wish to run away."

"No, I'm staying here. The Scythe will find me wherever I go, and besides, this is my home."

"I could counter attack."

"Not the Authority and not within a matter of hours." I firm my stance. "This is my plan. Will you help?"

He meets my gaze again before answering. "Yes, I will."

I exhale. "Excellent."

"Do you wish to also contact Chloe and Zoe? I understand they have skills that may be useful."

My eyes widen. "Who told you about them?" I hold my arm, palm forward, in a motion that means *hold on*. "Let me guess. Miss Edith told you?"

Thorne nods. "Before you arrived, Miss Edith was, uh, very forthcoming with information."

"Ugh, I don't want to know. Let's get to work."

"Let's."

Thorne then gives me a full smile. It's stunning. Little crinkle lines form by his eyes and everything. Plus, he has dimples. That's such a problem. I'm still not sure I believe all that stuff about us knowing each other in different dimensions. Even so, it's nice to have someone help me on this project.

Rubbing my forehead, I try to focus on something other than his grin. "I have some diagrams on my worktable. We can adapt them."

"Sounds like a plan." Thorne steps over to my ancient music player from RCM1. The thing is covered with scratch marks and food stains of indeterminate origin, but it works. "Music?" he asks.

"Yes, I need a beat when I work."

Thorne purses his lips and presses the *Play* button. Revival rock blares from the speaker. This stuff is super old, but since there's no music industry anymore, I'm happy to find whatever. The lead singer screeches out the lyrics to a remake of *Seven Nation Army*.

I wince. "Too loud?"

Another one of Thorne's dazzling smiles comes my way. "No, it's perfect."

I've never had a helper in my lab before. I'm not sure how it would be with anyone else, but for me and Thorne? It's like an intricate dance. He takes apart an exotic matter detector; I write code for a power burst.

We don't talk.

Music thrums through us.

Every once in a while, our hands or bodies brush, and I'd be a liar if I didn't say that I liked it. Thorne is solid everything.

Thought.

Muscle.

Confidence.

Everything Thorne touches ends up looking like a finished product, not a rough prototype. All in all, we make a pretty good team.

Some small voice in the back of my head says that after this prototype is built, he must leave to find Luci. Should I go with him? If we traveled together, I'd love to ask him a million questions about my parents, ECHO academy, his home planet, and this transcendent stuff. But I set aside those thoughts.

The prototype must come first.

The hours stream by, and before I know it, I'm installing my big red button atop the sealed briefcase. I'm a big believer of making it easy to know how my inventions get activated.

Inside the briefcase, the device is a careful weave of circuit boards and wires. Thorne and I ran a ton of diagnostic tests. No question about it. This thing will create a massive drift void at midnight on Saturday night at the Learning Squirrel High School.

What if the Authority can scan into the briefcase somehow and figure out how we built it? I hate to think that I'm helping Godwin. That said, I keep reminding how Thorne and I put in fail safes on our fail safes. They shouldn't be able to reverse engineer anything. In the end, I decide that there are no good choices here, only belief in my own judgment.

So I decide to trust myself as well.

When midnight comes around, the new security system talks through a freshly installed comm unit on the wall.

"Meimi, someone's approaching the back entrance."

The smooth voice startles me out of writing instructions for the Scythe. I punch off the music and turn to Thorne. "I got this. It's Fritz."

"I won't be far away."

I nod, close up the briefcase, and hightail it to the back door. The green rain is pounding now. When I open the back door, Fritz looks like a drowned swamp rat.

"You got it, ya?" The fake accent is back.

"Yes, instructions are here." I hand him a padded envelope and then turn over the briefcase. "I still hate the idea of Godwin having this."

"Don't worry, he won't use it. Just wants to run diagnostics." Fritz shoots me another look that seems guilty, but it's gone too quickly to be sure.

"Actually, that makes me *more* nervous than before. The Scythe said the Authority would actually use the thing. What's this really about?"

"Proof of your skills, Meimi. Don't worry, we'll all get rich off this."

Fritz shoves the briefcase and envelope under his coat and then turns away. I watch him trudge off into the night.

Not sure how I know this, but there's no question in my mind: Thorne is standing behind me, looking over my shoulder.

"I don't like this Fritz," he says.

I tilt my head, thinking. "I trust Fritz more than the Scythe."

And with that thought, all the adrenaline leaves my system. Suddenly, I've never felt more cold or tired. Shivers rack my spine.

"You need sleep," says Thorne.

At the mention of the word *sleep*, I let out the mother of all yawns. "Yes, I do." I turn around and realize how close Thorne and I now stand to each other.

This situation is all kinds of crazy. Stuff like this doesn't happen to people in general, or to me in particular. Thorne is an alien. He may seem familiar from my dreams, but what does that mean? If anything, it's probably a reason to trust him less.

At this point, I realize we've been staring at each other for a really long stretch of time. As in, birds could start chirping soon. Finally, I manage to speak again.

"What about you?" My voice comes out a hoarse whisper. "Do you need to sleep?"

"I don't require much rest." He takes a pointed step away from me. "Especially when I have work to do."

"Looking for Luci?"

"Among other things. I can't do anything until my gear is ready." He stares at me so intently, it's like he can see into my soul. Which is nutso.

I really need some sleep.

"Well, good night." I step toward my room, pause, and give Thorne a half wave.

"Sleep well," he intones.

I head off toward my bedroom, feeling his eyes on me the entire time.

Once I'm upstairs, I check that Mom's safe in bed. She looks so tiny, curled up on her side. Shifting beams of greenish moonlight seep through the window, casting her in an otherworldly glow. The look makes sense somehow. After all, Mom made a deal with someone from another world.

I tuck the threadbare blanket under her chin. What did my parents really do? Is any of this real? My head feels heavy with questions. Yet all my queries will have to wait until tomorrow. There isn't an inch of space left in my consciousness for anything but rest.

I slog my way to my room and tumble into bed. The moment my cheek presses against the cold pillow, my consciousness collapses into sleep.

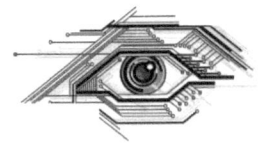

CHAPTER 17

THAT NIGHT, I dream of the Merciless.

In my vision, I lean against the kitchen counter. Miss Edith stands nearby, preparing one of her many cups of tea. Wisps of steam curl up from the liquid, forming odd shapes in the air.

A gentle hum sounds. Miss Edith and I share a confused look. The rumble quickly becomes deafeningly loud. The brick wall presses inwards. Long cracks form on the surface. My pulse skyrockets.

SMASH!

The wall implodes as a cone-shaped metallic vehicle spears through. A hoverdigger. The counter bursts under the force of the onslaught. Beams smash. Equipment shatters. The hoverdigger retreats, leaving a massive hole behind. Using that new entrance, warriors in black body armor pour into the room.

The Merciless.

Without hesitation, a Merciless warrior shoots Miss Edith in the chest. The gash gun tears through a huge swath of the sweet woman's torso. Miss Edith slumps to the ground, dead. I scream.

My dream world turns psychedelic and watery. Up is down. Doors morph and disappear. Somehow, I rush off and find Mom. Meanwhile the Merciless overrun the factory, smashing everything in sight. The warriors topple over the vats of old chemicals. Blood-red liquids seep across the floor, forming shapes that resemble skulls.

I sprint into Mom's room, but she's asleep and won't awaken. I shake her shoulders, screaming her name. She doesn't move, and that's when I realize it. Her sheets are thick with blood.

Mom's already dead.

"NO!"

I wake up screaming, my body covered in sweat. Thorne bursts through my door and pauses, his outline framed by green-tinted moonlight. The Sentient glisten on his arms, slipping down to his hands in a dark stream. Within seconds, they form a pair of short black swords.

I clutch my throat. "What are you doing?"

"Guarding you."

"From what?"

Thorne sniffs. "Do you want an alphabetized list?"

He looks so serious, I can't help but grin. "That would help, yes."

A glint of humor shines in Thorne's blue eyes. "Well, the letter A is for the *asshat* who took your prototype." Thorne twists his wrists; the Sentient-created swords retract into his skin. "Not sure if you can tell, but I didn't like that guy."

My smile widens. "Yeah, I got that."

Now that I've recovered from my shock, my brain finally processes what just happened. Thorne has been sitting outside my door, guarding me. Something warm unfurls inside my chest. It's been years since anyone spontaneously took care of me.

The situation is intoxicating.

Thrilling.

And frightening.

How can I rely on someone? What if something happens to Thorne like it did to Mom? I pull my covers up under my chin. "Thanks for checking in. I'll just ..." *sit here in the dark and freak out* "...go back to sleep."

Thorne slowly crosses the room. With gentle movements, he sits beside me on my tiny mattress. Reaching forward, he traces circles on the back of my hand with his pointer finger. I won't lie. It's incredibly soothing.

"Tell me what happened." Thorne's voice is deep and kind. His big blue eyes reflect sympathy and moonlight. "Why did you scream?"

"I had a nightmare."

"What did you see?"

"I was in the kitchen downstairs with Miss Edith. The Merciless showed up. Everyone was killed. Mom too."

"Rose is safe asleep. Miss Edith won't be here for hours. And I'll be right outside that door."

"You aren't treating this as just a dream."

"It's not." He lifts his gaze to mine. "It's a warning. My people place a lot of emphasis on dreams. And my Sentient are restless, which is another danger sign. But I merged some of them with the security system. If anything comes close, I'll know."

"Ah, your alphabetized list. A is for asshat."

"B is for Bad guys." He runs his finger along my jawline. The touch is electric, sending a shiver across my shoulders. "You need to rest ..." He pauses, tilting his head. A frown mars his handsome face.

"What's wrong?"

"Information is coming in from my Sentient. The Merciless are approaching the factory. I can clearly hear their conversation."

Every nerve ending in my body seems to light on fire. "Mom."

"No, they're not after her. They're talking about you." He pauses. "Once they cross into the factory, my systems will scan their tech more deeply. I'll get a better read on their plans."

"The Merciless have only one plan. Shoot people."

A smash sounds downstairs as windows break. The security system wails a few long sirens before falling silent. Voices echo through the factory. I recognize one tone above all the others.

"Ya, ya," says Fritz. "You'll find her upstairs. Second room on the left."

A jolt of shock moves through my limbs. "This is more than the Merciless." I set my hand on my throat. "Fritz and the Scythe sold me out."

Dark light glistens on his Thorne's skin. This is just like what happened to me with the Lacerator, right before our minds connected.

Thorne is linking to someone as well. Or something.

"I have access to their tech." Thorne rises from the cot, his face angry as thunder. "They have plans for you, Meimi."

Thorne and I stare at each other in the moonlight. Downstairs on the factory floor, a chorus of bootfalls echo, along with the click of weapons being unholstered.

The Merciless are here.

I whip off my covers. "I have to get Mom."

"Go to Rose, and they'll shoot her just to reach you. They don't care about your mother. They won't kill you because they plan to—"

Standing, I place my fingertips on his lips. "I don't want to know. All I want is for Mom to be safe. Please, Thorne. Guard her as you would me."

"Don't ask me this."

"If there's some connection between us, you already know the truth. I won't be moved."

Thorne cups my face in his hands. "Then let me help you in another way. Can you trust in that?"

Our shared connection returns. Thorne's emotions flow through my soul. I don't need to look down and see the now-familiar blue particles. Instead, I soak in the feelings.

The searing pain of worry.

Rock-solid conviction.

Raw honesty.

"Yes, Thorne." My voice comes out rough and low. "I trust you."

Thorne closes his eyes, and even in the dim moonlight, I can see his skin change color. Not just particles, but every inch of him is now colored in azure.

"You're blue."

"Yes."

"You really, really are an alien."

A small smile quirks his mouth again. "And you're not frightened of me."

"I should be." In fact, I should scream and run right now, and for multiple reasons. Maybe it's my dreams. Or the intensity of Throne's emotions. Or something else I'm too afraid to name.

Whatever it is, I can't help but stare at his mouth.

"Never be frightened of me, Rosa Meimifloria Archer, my glorious girl named after the drift rose." Thorne leans in closer. His breath fans across my lips. "I'll do whatever it takes to keep you safe. And for me, my people, a kiss can connect our consciousness in special ways." He gently moves his mouth across mine.

Black, silver, and blue light now flare across Throne's azure skin. The same colors shine from me as well. Deep in my soul, new links form. Energies entwine. Psychological cogs connect and spin. Warmth and affection spread.

I break the kiss, breathless. The light from our skin dies down. The azure hue disappears from Thorne.

"What was that?" I ask.

"The only way I can keep you safe." Thorne's mouth thins to a determined line. "Although it will mean a battle with my father."

"Over me?"

Thorne nods.

Fresh panic streams through my veins. "Don't do that. I'm not worth it."

"That's where you're wrong, Meimi. You're remarkable."

"Why? Because I build prototypes?"

"No, because you've a true heart, stellar mind, and fighting spirit. I'd tear apart any number of universes for you. You may find this hard to believe, but I already have."

A flicker of my old dreams appears. This time, I remember one word clearly. It's the same one Thorne spoke a few hours and a million years ago.

"Transcendent," I whisper.

Thorne frames my face with his fingertips. The touch of his skin is rough and sweet, all at once. "That's right."

Moving up on tiptoe, I touch my mouth to his. The kiss quickly deepens. Bootfalls sound on the metal staircase outside. *The Merciless.* Thorne and I break apart. My heart cracks.

That might be our last kiss.

Thorne gives me a sad smile. "When the time is right, that kiss will help you remember." Stepping over to the wall, Thorne sets his hands against the concrete. "And until then, your mother will be safe."

Sentient shimmer on Thorne's hands. The tiny particles with spread out from his arms, creating an oval on the wall. For a heartbeat, the concrete shimmers with silver light. Then an opening appears in the wall, connecting my room to Mom's.

Relief and fear tear through me in equal measure. Thorne will enter Mom's room and make sure she's okay. But I'll be alone.

Thorne steps through the newly-made exit in the wall. A moment later, the concrete returns to its regular gray.

There's no sign of the Sentient.

The wall is smooth and unbroken once more.

Thorne is gone and it breaks my heart.

Fritz stomps across the threshold, followed by four Merciless warriors. My pulse goes through the stratosphere. He points at my nose. "That's her, ya."

My gaze automatically shifts to the spot where Thorne left to guard Mom. There's still no sign of him. I repeat words in my mind like a mantra.

Thorne got away. Mom will be safe.
And Fritz is a dick.

I glare at my one-time handler. "So you're pawning me off to the Merciless. How could you?"

"There was just too much money in it." Fritz drops the fake accent for once, and I take that as a sign that I'm in deep trouble indeed. "The things you can do, Meimi. You've gotten too big for even me and the Scythe to control."

One of the Merciless steps forward, but Fritz holds out his arm, stopping the warrior in his tracks. "Let me explain things to her. It will go more easily that way." Fritz steps closer. "The Authority is taking you, but don't worry. You're far too valuable to be killed."

"And my mother?"

"You already know the answer to that question, Meims. Once we're done with you, we'll euthanize her. That should have happened long ago."

Fritz reaches behind him. When his arm comes back out, he's holding a syringe with blue liquid. There's only one substance that particular shade—the very tranquilizer I'm immune to. A glimmer of a plan appears in my mind. Maybe I can fake being passed out. There's always opportunity in the unexpected.

I lift my chin and keep right on glaring at him. "We had a deal."

"A deal means equal parties, Meimi." Fritz's eyes widen with sadness. "That's never how it was with us." He snaps his fingers, and four Merciless guards leap toward me, holding me in place. Something pinches my neck.

A needle.

It's the blue fluid.

They're giving me an injection.

My head turns murky. It takes a lot of concentration, but I'm able to speak once more. "Nice try."

"Because you think you're immune," says Fritz. "But not from this level of dose."

My breath catches. Of course, Fritz would've tracked that about me.

"Don't worry, Meims. When the Merciless are done, you'll have a new identity, memory, sponsor family, everything. This will be better for you. Rose was holding you down."

My head feels wobbly on my shoulders. The tranqs are kicking in. Even so, I manage to stay upright as a new figure steps into my bedroom.

Doctor Godwin.

Oh, crap.

Godwin raises a briefcase in his hands. And not just any briefcase, it's the one that holds my latest prototype. "Did you build this?"

It's hard to stay vertical. Somehow, I manage it. "No."

"Don't listen to her," counters Fritz. "That thing is set for her high school and it's covered in her DNA. It's like I told you right after the massacre at RCM1. Meimi is brilliant. She can get you what you need. You saw what she did at RCM1."

"I only witnessed a petulant child who knows how to toss a chem dart," says Godwin.

"So?" counters Fritz. "That's why we sent you the enhancer as proof.

But you still weren't convinced. Which is why Meimi built you this prototype in less than a day." Fritz folds his arms over his chest. "It's pretty clear to me that she's what you need. Or are you just sore that she knocked you out? Big bad doctor getting dosed with tranqs?"

"I'm not sore." Godwin's nostrils flare. "I do need a drift scientist."

"Like I said, that's Meimi," declares Fritz.

Much as I hate to admit it, Fritz is trying to help me. His efforts are demented and loaded with self-interest, but I can't deny that it's also keeping me alive.

"We'll see," says Godwin in his sinister whisper. "I need to see her perform in a controlled environment over time. No tricks. Bring in her sponsors."

A couple steps into my bedroom. My head turns fuzzier than ever before. Maybe it's the drugs, but I didn't notice their faces when the pair first entered the room. And now? Their backs are to me.

"Meet your new charge," Godwin says to the couple. "You'll sponsor her for the summer. If her work pleases me, she can attend ECHO Academy. I might even bring her into my plans with the Lacerator."

The woman turns to face me. All the breath seems to leave my body. Chills run across my skin.

This can't be right.

No, no, no.

It's Luci.

My sister looks as she always did: white-blonde hair, thin frame, and icy blue eyes. For the first time I can remember, she glares at me with a look of pure hatred.

"I told you already," snaps Luci. "Meimi can't help you with drift science. She's useless."

I stumble backward, her words hitting me like fists. The back of my legs slam against my cot. I crouch down to sit.

This can't be Luci.

Here.

Hating me.

Godwin rounds on my sister. "What part of my instructions were unclear?"

Luci frowns. "But—"

"Don't test me, Luci. You're only here because you're her sister and every other attempt we've made to recruit this girl had failed. We ask her to volunteer at school? She's not interested. The Scythe request to be her sponsor? He gets turned down. Now it's up to you two." He eyes Luci from head to toe. "You and your husband are the worst sponsor parents in our system. Do you want to keep the credits rolling in? Fix this."

Luci stomps her foot. "I already told you, Meimi can't do it."

"You better hope she can," says Godwin. "Or you'll pay the price."

For the first time, the guy speaks. "Hey, she's not *my* sister."

"My threat goes for both of you." Godwin stares at the Merciless guards. For a moment, I think he might order them to fire on Luci. Instead, Godwin slides the briefcase under his arm and marches out of the room.

Good riddance.

Now, it's the man who turns around to face me. My heart sinks. Sure enough, it's Josiah. He reminds me of a shabby version of the Scythe, but with everything out of place. Uneven features. Overly greased back hair. Cheap frayed suit. Josiah scans me with what can only be described as a leer. "You've grown up, Meimi."

It's the leer that pushes me over the edge. How is this guy my new sponsor father? I turn to my sister. "Why are you doing this?"

My sister doesn't reply, only stalks closer. "Dad loved roses, you know that? It all started because Mom's name is Rose. Then he named me after the white rose, Luciae. You're named after the drift rose, Meimifloria."

The drugs hit my nervous system, hard. I crumple onto my side, the mattress feeling impossibly cold under my skin.

"And for a while, our family's life was nothing but roses, too," continues Luci. "That is, until *you* came along. Dad used to make good money. Mom did, too. We were set until *you* ruined everything. But now, things are finally turning around. Godwin's setting you up, and I'll be the beneficiary. And the best part? You'll have your memory wiped, so you won't recall any of this conversation."

This has to be the drugs. After all, I was just starting to accept that Luci was a little entitled and Josiah was a tad creepy. But this? Luci loathes me? Wants to ruin me? What did I ever do to her?

Luci looms over my bed and grins. "You'll repay your debt to me, Pumpkin. I'll make sure of it."

Spots appear in my vision. A metallic taste takes over my mouth. I don't have long to stay alert. And based on what Luci said, not much time remains for me to stay Meimi. Final thoughts appear before the drugs fully pull me under.

No, you're wrong, Luci. That kiss from Thorne means I'll remember everything. And I'm not the one who'll pay.

My enemies will.

—*The End*—

The adventure continues with UMBRA, book 2 of the Dimension Drift. Read on for a sample chapter!

Experience Thorne's point of view in UMBRA!

ALSO BY CHRISTINA BAUER

Try ANGELBOUND, the kick-ass paranormal romance with more than 1 million copies sold!

FAIRY TALES OF THE MAGICORUM

A modern fairy tale that *USA Today* calls a 'must-read!' Check out WOLVES AND ROSES!

PIXIELAND DIARIES tells the story of sassy pixie Calla and 'her' elf prince, Dare.

Medieval mages ... Slow-burn love ... And heart-pounding action! Check out the BEHOLDER series!

"Wish to travel the omniverse? First try leaping off a hovercraft without a power chute. Should you live, then you might survive in alternate realities as well." – Beauregard the Great, *Instructions for Visiting Parallel Worlds*

Nine minutes.

That's how long before this planet implodes.

I'm talking about a version of Earth that supports thousands of cities. Millions of buildings. Billions of people. Not to mention what's almost beyond counting. Like photographs. Sunflowers. Bowling trophies. Baby carriages. As of this moment, I'm the only barrier between all that and instant annihilation.

Welcome to my Tuesday.

I'm Thorne Oxblood, and I fight inter-dimensional disasters.

For my current mission, I'm at placelet 92.248.908, planet X3894-B, strand BT704.35, and branch point 1T.783-50E. The locals have a simpler name for this location, though. *Clyde's Gym.* Over the last hour, I've memorized every inch of this space, searching for the *schism*—meaning the inter-dimensional breaking point—that could tear this world apart. Nothing has shown itself yet. Nervous energy corkscrews up my shoulders and neck. *What am I missing?* For the umpteenth time, I inspect the gym.

Large, square space with concrete walls? *Check.*

Rickety slats in a worn-out floor? *Check.*

Faded girly calendars everywhere? *Odd decoration, but it's not my gym. And check.*

Points of access? *Three.* Main entrance up-front, an office side door, and a small emergency exit along the back wall. Since I arrived, no one's entered or left.

Huge letter K glowing on the ceiling? *Check.* This is something only I can see, and it means my family's arch-enemy, the Komandir, stopped by this gym at some point. Not as helpful a fact as one might think. It still doesn't show me where the schism is hiding.

Humans? *Nine.* Two boxers pound away in the sparring ring. Another six guys slam into punching bags, lift weights or jump rope. One teenage girl scribbles on papers behind the door marked *office.* Then, there's me. To the humans, I'm just an eighteen-year-old in gray sweats. Nothing about my muscular build, short hair, and blue eyes screams, *this guy's an alien.*

But I am from another world. *Umbra.*

And as an Umbran, my body stores tiny cybernetic organisms called sentient. These minute creatures enable me to guard the omniverse, which is the universe of universes. Tonight's mission marks my seventy-first rescue. For the record, my sentient are extra jacked up at this point. They keep sending me mental images of this planet exploding in a silent shower of blinding light.

Not for the first time, I try to calm them. *I got it,* I whisper in my mind. *There's trouble at Clyde's Gym.*

Another explosion image follows. *Not helping.*

I rub my temples and try to focus. *Think through the problem, Thorne.* Since I saw the glowing K, I've assumed the Komandir are behind the trouble here. But maybe the symbol is a distraction. Perhaps something else is at work. After all, these humans could be about to develop drift science, which is the ability to open alternate realities. Once you can visit other worlds, it's easier to implode your own. Drift science would also explain why my sentient keep sending images of exploding planets instead of pics showing Doc Zykin, the Komandir assassin.

Closing my eyes, I reach out to my sentient. *Is drift science the real problem here?*

In reply, my sentient show me beauty queens jumping up and down after winning a pageant. It's their way of saying, *yes already.* Amazing how, even though they can't speak, my sentient still manage to be sarcastic.

Fresh scenes flood my mind. This time, my sentient review my last mission.

I stand in a huge white space. A sign for New Cosmos University hangs above me; equipment covers the floor all around. There are tall monoliths with computer arrays, a patchwork of workstations, and round databots that zoom through the air. I stand at the drift science station, dressed in a white lab coat. It took me two weeks to infiltrate this place as a research student. After that, I spent days hacking into university systems so anyone with Umbran DNA would be immune to security. Yet the real time-suck on this mission has been my target, Helen Robbins. She's whip-smart with long black hair, cocoa skin, and a gaze that could melt titanium.

She thinks I'm up to something.

She's right.

Trouble is, my secret agenda is to stop this version of Earth from imploding. For that to happen, Helen must ace her latest set of drift science calculations. How do I know her calcs are key? My sentient keep making her data pad glow red. For weeks, I've tried to help her, but she keeps blocking any attempts at conversation. My only chance is that the school board wants fresh numbers today.

"How's it going?" I ask. "I know you're on a deadline."

Helen presses her tablet against her chest. "What's it to you?"

"I want to help. That's it. Honestly."

Helen pauses. Little by little, she starts handing me her datapad.

At last.

I could cheer.

Behind me, the lab door thuds open. My brother Justice bursts into the room. He's a bulky figure dressed in cowboy boots, a black T-shirt, jeans and a Stetson. In some kind of nod to science, he holds a pocket protector in his left hand. He stomps over to my side.

"How's it going, little bro?" Justice closes his eyes. I know what he's doing—accessing his sentient. "Guess you met the smartest filly in this here lab." Justice increases intensity as he says 'smartest filly.' I get it. Justice means that his sentient pinpointed Helen as the target for this mission. Sadly, my brother already has a loud and gravelly voice. Upping the volume only makes the words 'smartest filly' boom through the chamber. Everyone stops working to stare.

My jaw muscles lock in frustration. Justice came here to check on me, clear and simple. Did it take me a few days to determine Helen was my target? Sure. I don't have Justice's power over sentient, so I figured it out on my own. Now, I'm finally finishing my work here, and my brother shows up to 'help.'

He could ruin everything.

I look to Helen. She's clasped the datapad so tightly against her torso, the girl's knuckles flare white. "That's your brother?" she asks, her face scrunched in disbelief.

I pinch the bridge of my nose. "Yup. Can you ignore him?"

"I don't know." Helen takes a half-step backward. "He's really really really big."

Justice tips the brim of his Stetson. "Thank you, sugar."

"Wasn't a complement," deadpans Helen. Justice keeps right on smiling. He's

convinced every woman loves him. Mostly because he's the most eligible bachelor on Umbra.

I step closer to Helen. "Please. You only deal with him once. I've got him for the rest of my life."

Helen pauses, then cracks a smile. "I've an older sister, too. Name's Polly." She hands over the datapad. "Poll's a lot like your brother."

"Is that right, now?" Justice flashes Helen a thousand-watt smile. "Is this Polly of yours all charm and sunshine, just like me?"

Helen chuckles. "Nope, she's more of a busybody. Thinks I can't do anything without her."

"So." Justice puffs out his lower lip. "Not like me."

While Helen and Justice chat, I scan the datapad, make a few notes, and hand it back. "Your results from the dark matter tests are off," I explain. The data comes another team, and I'm not surprised their work sucks. That group's more interested in clubbing than science. "Rerun the tests yourself and your calcs will be fine."

Helen scans the screen. "Thanks. If these numbers were off, it could have caused an explosion."

"Through space and time," adds Justice.

"Thanks," I tell my brother. "But I'm handling this." Which in family-speak translates to: shut the hell up.

Helen gives me the side eye. "How could you know those tests looked wrong? This is all new. No one's seen proper results yet."

Justice taps his temple. "My little brother here's a thinker. He's got to be, considering how he's low on sentient and all." Justice closes his eyes for a moment. "Good news. Now those numbers are put to rights, this here universe is safe again. Nice how things work out, huh?"

Helen frowns. "Did you say sentient?"

"Yes indeedy," replies Justice. My brother then turns to me. "Speaking of sentient, did you catch how mine said our work here is done? We aced this mission together, little bro."

"I caught that part, yes." I'd add that Justice did no actual work to ace said mission, but that will only lead to more humiliating speeches about my weakness with sentient.

Justice slaps his hand on my shoulder. "Let's get back to Umbra."

Helen's brows lift. "Umbra?"

I shake my head. "Oh, it's definitely time to leave."

The memory replay ends. It's obvious why my sentient showed me that scene. In Helen's world, fixing drift science was the key to saving her planet. The same could be true here as well. Even so, Helen's mission lasted for weeks and took place in a laboratory. This time, I've only got eight more minutes and a gymnasium.

Not gonna lie.

I'm at a loss here.

The main door swings open; five teenage guys step inside. All of them sport pomade-slick hair, white T-shirts, and cuffed jeans. *Classic greasers.* Which makes sense. After all, this parallel Earth broke off from the prime reality sometime in the 1950's. Branch worlds often get stuck on their exit point.

The tallest in the group pauses just inside the door. He's got a square face, a flat nose, and a great swoosh of blond hair. His stocky body seems ready to burst from his leather bomber jacket. A smaller teen pulls at the tall guy's elbow.

"Axel," he begins.

"Quiet, Runt."

"The name's Ralph," squeaks the little guy.

"You're whatever I call you." Axel elbows the smaller kid in gut. Ralph gasps in pain, but he doesn't fight back. *Interesting.* So whatever this group is, Axel is both their leader and a total dick. Not good. Axel's beady eyes narrow as he inspects the room.

He's looking for someone.

Beep... beep...

My earpiece lets out a soft tone that only I can hear. Based on the rhythm, I already know who's calling. *Justice.*

"Accept inbound comm," I say.

My brother's gravelly voice echoes across the line. "You've got less than seven minutes left, little brother. Vamoose."

"Not an option," I declare. "My mission isn't over."

"Then I'm coming after you. Now."

Right. Justice would be here already if I hadn't hidden my placelet data. After the disaster with Helen, I figured out that trick.

"Any news for me?" I ask.

"The S-Man got us some info."

By S-Man, Justice means Slate, our youngest brother. Together, the three of us make up the royal family for Umbra. As Emperor of the Omniverse, our father Cole wields the all-powerful Crown Sentient, while Slate's abilities focus on visions and knowledge.

"This Earth is developing drift science tech," continues Justice.

"My sentient already showed me that." In my head, images of cheering crowds appear from my sentient. They rarely beat out Slate in getting me news.

"Come on, now." Justice sighs. "You know what that means—most worlds destroy themselves once they reach this stage. Why save this planet?"

"Universes are born and die all the time," I counter. "Sentient pick which ones to save. Not us. You know that." While I chat with Justice, I can't help but notice how Axel keeps glaring at the office door. Something tells me I should take another look in there. "Unless you've got other news, I'm signing off."

"Hold your horses, now. Be reasonable. You're not like me and Slate."

My voice lowers. "I'm aware."

Both Justice and Slate are far stronger with sentient than I am. Hell, there are grandmas on my planet with more sentient power than I carry. And I get what Justice means. In this mission, he and Slate could escape an imploding planet much faster than I ever could. *Which is why I must succeed here or else.* I'm about to say precisely that when something happens.

The side office door opens. My sentient stop sending images of cheering crowds. Instead, fresh sensations course through me.

A buzz of excitement.

The pang of anticipation.

A rock-solid weight of willpower.

These aren't my emotions, though. It's all coming from my sentient. This is their way of saying, *the schism is close by.*

"Hold on," I tell Justice.

A girl steps through the newly-opened side door. She's the same teenager I counted before, only now I can catch a better look. She's young, red-haired, and wearing a poodle skirt. The name Emma is embroidered on her sweater. A pile of books and papers lie cradled in her arms. To my eyes, the documents glow with crimson light. As with Helen, my sentient are telling me that I found it.

The schism.

At last, this is familiar territory. If this mission is like Helen's, then those papers will carry drift science calculations. Once I fix a few numbers, then the schism will close. I check my watch once more.

Five minutes.

More than enough time.

Emma steps out the emergency back door. Axel stalks along after her, his thin tongue flickering hungrily over his heavy lips. I pause. On second thought, there may be more work here than simply fixing calculations. Axel and his buddies might put up a fight.

I take it back. That's a lot for five minutes.

Suddenly, long cracks form in the gym walls and ceiling. Red light peeps out through the fissures, casting odd patterns across the space. My pulse speeds. I've seen this effect before, and it means one thing.

This world is pulling apart.

On reflex, I scan the nearby faces. Everyone still goes about their business. Punching. Jumping. Lifting. The breaks are only visible to me, thanks to my sentient. Doesn't make them any less real, though.

"I got it," I tell Justice. "The schism centers on a girl named Emma; she just moved into an alley. Some guys trailed her. I'll go after them."

"No way." Justice's voice takes on a frantic note. "A bunch of guys sneak into a dark alley and you're following? You've no idea what kind of tech they're packing. I'm coming in to help you."

I prowl across the gym floor. More fissures appear beneath my feet. "Justice, I got this."

"No! Your hero complex is plum out of control. Give me your exact placelet location and—"

I click the earpiece off, ending our connection. As I march toward the back door, my brother's words echo through my mind.

Your hero complex is plum out of control.

Justice is wrong.

I don't have a hero complex.

It's more of a death wish.

My brothers and I make up the royal family of Umbra. We're expected to wield exceptional powers with sentient. Slate and Justice do; I don't. That makes me the chipped jewel in an otherwise-perfect crown.

I'm the extra prince.

Weak brother.

Unworthy royal.

Someone to be pitied as he's pushed aside.

Fuck that.

With each mission, I get one step closer to either proving myself a true royal ... or checking out of this game entirely. The question always hangs over me. Am I a real prince or a dead fool? Yanking on the back door, I step out into the darkened alley.

Maybe tonight's when things get settled, one way or another.

⌑

—End Of Sample—

Order UMBRA today!

NEW APPENDIX OF TOTALLY AWESOME GOODIES

WELCOME TO THIS NEW APPENDIX!

I've added lots of extra stuff here in order to celebrate the release of new covers for my Dimension Drift series! Check them out below:

Say it with me: *ooooh, aaaaaah!*

Now, you may wonder: *what's behind the new covers?*
Good question, you.
There are my five reasons why I did this.

One. The 'I Gotta Be Me' Cover

With the original covers, the first three had a theme of characters running through walls. Then the fourth book, ECHO ACADEMY, did it own thing. It was walls, walls, walls and... WTF? That bugged me.

Two. I Like Visuals

Reviewers often say that reading my books is like watching a movie in their heads. And hey, that's what it's like when I write them, too! Even after the books are launched, I'm still picturing the story and how to enhance it. All of which leads to item number three...

Three. More Books A-Coming

Great news! I plan on adding two more books to the series, namely JUSTICE and SLATE. As it was before, the cover design template wasn't really expandable to those guys. After all, you can only run through so many walls before things starts to get repetitive. This new format will fit in the two new titles perfectly. Yay!

Four. Getting Less Literal

The first covers represented actual scenes from the books. It was fun at the time, but I think it's a little limiting in the long run. Plus, this series is science fiction which I think lends itself to more *suggestive versus literal* design. The new look should give you an idea of the book's themes without getting too specific.

Four. Reader Goodies

Recently, I added an extra appendix to SLIPPERS AND THIEVES, a title from my Fairy Tales of the Magicorum series. Readers really liked it—and I love making you all happy—so the new covers were a good excuse to add in more content here as well.

All in all, I truly hope you enjoy these extra goodies... and please keep an eye out for a release date on JUSTICE and SLATE!

Best,
Christina Bauer, Author

WHY I REWROTE SCYTHE

FOR THOSE OF you who follow my work, you know that I rewrote and relaunched SCYTHE.

Here's how it all went down.

After fifteen books, I thought my writing process seems set. Rock solid. Then comes SCYTHE and the Dimension Drift series. I get an idea: how about doing two prequel novellas before book one proper? No biggie, right?

Wrong.

Here's the deal. I outline the entire series. Then I write prequel novellas one and two, aka SCYTHE and UMBRA. So far, so good. After that, I dive into book one, ALIEN MINDS, aaaaaaaaaaand the writer part of my personality decides it's time to change a bunch of stuff in the prequels.

Trouble is, SCYTHE's already published.

A fight ensues. The combatants? Author Me versus Business Me. It goes a little something like this ...

Author Me: I shall rewrite SCYTHE.

Business Me: Forget it! We just released that novella. No one changes stuff that's already live. Drop that idea right now.

Author Me: (Sticks fingers in ears) La la la, I can't hear you.

Two weeks pass. The la la la-ing never ends. Nothing gets written. Deadlines loom. Panic ensues. Business Me caves.

. . .

Business Me: Fine, do whatever you want.
   Writer Me: Mwah hah hah!

Therefore, I rewrote and relaunched a new version of SCYTHE and it's exactly what Writer Me wants. And Business Me admits that the novella kicks WAY more ass this way.

:::crosses fingers:::

I hope you think so, too!

How do I create a book like SCYTHE? Here are my top three engines for writing urban fantasy!

One. Go back three generations

When I start world building, I force myself to go back three generations and think up the backstory that got the world to the present day. In UMBRA, there's a new authoritarian government that just took over ruling the United Americas. Why did this happen? I'll outline all this, but the detail never shows up on the page.

A big thing from this back-planning was the lack of new manufacturing in my version of Earth. If you wanted a shirt, you need to go find it in a landfill. So the main character from book one, SCYTHE, worked in what's called a reclamation center, which is a fancy way of saying she picked through garbage for a living.

Two. Get inside the alien's head

The main character in UMBRA is an alien from another planet called (you guessed it) Umbra. I thought for a long time about making the planet super-high tech and all stainless steel, but I don't think that's what a futuristic society would really want. I decided that when you've been incredibly high tech for a while, then you're want to pretend you're back in simpler times. So the planet Umbra is made to look like the Wild West, but is actually made from tiny filaments that are packed with technology. Touch a wall and it turns into long fibers that part to allow you to leave, that kind of thing.

Three: It's not fantasy for your characters

One of the hardest things about intense world building is the desire to shout on every page, guess how I solved *this* problem? Want to know the history behind *that* character? But my characters aren't interested in yelling their backstories, they simply want to live their lives. So the trick is placing in enough info dumps that the reader knows about this foreign world, but not so many that it pulls away from the narrative.

So there you have it – the three biggest factors I consider when building fantasy worlds like SCYTHE!

CHARACTERS I'D LOVE TO INTERVIEW

As part of the launch tour for my book SCYTHE, the awesome folks at *Declarations Of A Fangirl* have asked me for a top 10 list, so I decided to share the top ten characters I'd love to interview. But then, my list got blabby so I cut it down to five. Hopefully the Fangirl folks have a sense of humor and some patience, because here goes!

1. The Balrog, *Lord of the Rings*

My interview: "Look, I get how you think Gandalf woke you up in Moria and that got your demonic self mightily pissed off. So then, you went out cracking your whip and showing some attitude. Fine. But why not just let it end with 'get off my lawn' or the equivalent? Why fight freaking Gandalf until you got your molten ass smote against a mountainside? I feel like there's more here to know. Also: were you wearing fuzzy bunny slippers during the battle? The text is unclear on that point." (Note: the text is unclear. Seriously.)

2. Hermione, all Harry Potter books

"Let's get into a little trust tree here and talk. Don't you really-really-REALLY want to be with Harry? I mean, Ron is nice but he's ... *Ron*. You'd have *weasel* in your last name forever. Not that it's a deal breaker but it's a point of consideration. Plus, I feel like you're just not doing your full due diligence. Would it hurt to have just one little kiss to test things out with Harry and then report back? Go ahead and do it now. I'll wait."

. . .

3. Vivian (Julia Roberts), *Pretty Woman*

"From the start of the movie, you wanted to go back to school. So awesome and interesting!!! But for what? Cleary, it wasn't a Masters in Advanced Prostitution, so where did you want to direct all your non-passionate passion? And did you ever go back to school after driving away with Edward (Richard Gere)? I'm dying to know. Personally, I think there should be a follow-up movie where you get your MBA and run companies together with Edward. Discuss."

4. Bella, *Twilight*

"Awesome book 1, but I do have a little nit to pick. So while your honey is off fighting the big bad, you're totally scared. Makes sense. But cowering is just not a good look on anybody. How about a few shouts of 'great job' or 'on your left!' You could also throw a shoe or something, just putting it out there. Thoughts?"

5. Anastasia, *50 Shades of Grey*

"It's just us girls here. I get having fun, but honestly? How many gallons of cranberry juice did you guzzle through that relationship because OW."

That's it! My top five character interviews. And yes, I do keep a running list of these things.

STANDARD APPENDIX OF STUFF
THAT'S STILL PRETTY COOL

IF YOU ENJOYED THIS BOOK...

...Please consider leaving a review, even if it's just a line or two. Every bit truly helps.

Plus I have it on good authority that every time you review an indie author, somewhere an angel gets a mocha latte.

For reals.

And angels need their caffeine, too.

ACKNOWLEDGMENTS

If you're reading my freaking acknowledgements, chances are, I should thank you for something. So, for the record: you are awesome, dear reader.

That said, huge and heartfelt thanks must go out to my husband and son for their rock-solid support. Being an author means a lot of early mornings, late nights, long weekends, and never-ending patience. You two are the best guys in the universe, period.

After that, I must thank the extensive network of reviewers, friends and colleagues who helped me build my writing chops in general. Gracias.

Finally, deep affection goes out to my late, much loved, and dearly missed Aunt Sandy and Uncle Henry. You saw the writer in me, always. Thank you, first and last.

ABOUT CHRISTINA BAUER

Christina Bauer thinks that fantasy books are like bacon: they just make life better. All of which is why she writes romance novels that feature demons, dragons, wizards, witches, elves, elementals, and a bunch of random stuff that she brainstorms while riding the Boston T. Oh, and she includes lots of humor and kick-ass chicks, too. Christina lives in Newton, MA with her husband, son, and semi-insane golden retriever, Ruby.

Stalk Christina on Social Media

Blog:
http://monsterhousebooks.com/blog/category/christina

Facebook:
https://www.facebook.com/authorBauer/

Instagram:
https://www.instagram.com/christina_cb_bauer/

Twitter:
@CB_Bauer

VLOG:
https://tinyurl.com/Vlogbauer

Web site:
www.bauersbooks.com

COMPLIMENTARY BOOK

Get a FREE book when you sign up for Christina's newsletter: https://tinyurl.com/bauersbooks

BEVERLY HILLS VAMPIRE

A NOVELLA BY CHRISTINA BAUER